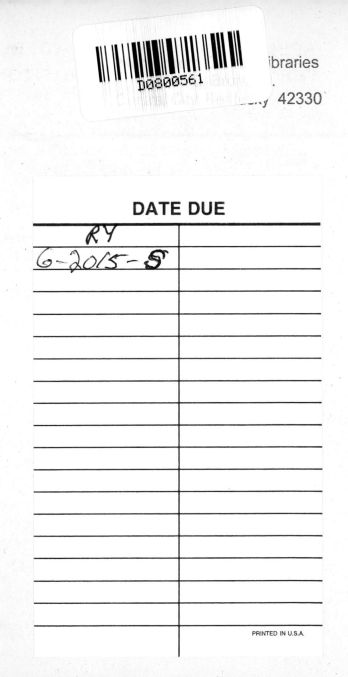

DATE DUE

RY
6-2015-5

THE LAND OF LOST DREAMS

Unlucky gambler Sebastian Ford owes everyone money. When Denver Fetterman calls in his debt, Ford's only option is to flee, offering his services as a guide to a wagon train of settlers. However, to repay his debts he must lead them into Hangman's Gulch, where they are to be ambushed — and, to make sure he doesn't renege, Fetterman's stalwart debt collector Chuck Kelley will go with him. When Sebastian sides with the settlers, however, only hot lead will get him out of trouble . . .

SCOTT CONNOR

---◆---

THE LAND OF LOST DREAMS

Complete and Unabridged

LINFORD
Leicester

First published in Great Britain in 2013 by
Robert Hale Limited
London

First Linford Edition
published 2014
by arrangement with
Robert Hale Limited
London

A catalogue record for this book is available
from the British Library.

ISBN 978–1–4448–2175–8

Published by
F. A. Thorpe (Publishing)
Anstey, Leicestershire

Set by Words & Graphics Ltd.
Anstey, Leicestershire
Printed and bound in Great Britain by
T. J. International Ltd., Padstow, Cornwall

This book is printed on acid-free paper

Prologue

Sebastian Ford considered Dawson Breen over the mountain of chips. The other two players had folded, but they had stayed to watch the showdown, as had most of the customers in the Bonanza House's private gaming room.

As he had done before when he'd bluffed, Sebastian tapped two fingers on the table. Although, as Dawson was the owner of the Bonanza House, the most opulent gaming house in Eureka, he doubted he'd be so naïve as to let that tactic concern him.

They were playing five-card stud with two cards placed face down and three cards lying face up. On the table both men had two kings exposed with Sebastian having an accompanying ace and Dawson a nine.

Dawson had bet with confidence from the start, suggesting his first card

1

in the hole was another nine. He had also watched Sebastian's reactions closely and had surely judged it unlikely he had received another ace.

Accordingly, Dawson pushed all his chips into the centre of the table.

'Shall we end this?' he asked.

'This is the right hand to end the night,' Sebastian said. He shoved his chips into the pile, letting sixteen thousand dollars ride on the hand.

Dawson sat back and calmly locked his hands behind his head. Behind him the watching customers inched forward.

As he'd probably bet more on this one hand than he'd wagered on every other hand of poker he'd played in his entire life, Sebastian struggled to maintain his confident demeanour. So, to calm himself, he considered the milling people. His attention was drawn to one man, who stood at the bar with his hat drawn down low, nursing a whiskey.

Sebastian wasn't sure why this man had intrigued him until he realized that he was the only one there who wasn't watching the game. But then, as if the man had picked up on Sebastian's interest, he put his glass down.

Then he wove through the throng to stand at Dawson's shoulder with his legs planted well apart and his face hidden in the shadow cast by his hat. Guns weren't allowed in the Bonanza House, but this man slipped his hand beneath his jacket with the practised ease of a hired gun.

The faint rustle of cloth and the shuffling of feet as the watching customers edged away from this man made Dawson smile. Then he leaned forward and, as he had made the last raise, turned over his first hole card to reveal the nine of diamonds.

Sebastian and Dawson locked gazes. Then Dawson flipped over his second card. Dawson's eyes widened slightly with a look of triumph that told Sebastian everything he needed to know about the card.

But he still looked down and

confirmed his opponent did have a third nine.

'Full house, nines over kings,' Dawson said. 'Only two aces can beat my hand and I don't reckon you've got them.'

Sebastian turned over his first hole card revealing the ace of spades, making Dawson's right eye twitch while the hired gun edged forward for a short pace.

Then Sebastian flicked over his second card.

1

The Pioneer Saloon was the cheapest and dirtiest saloon in the two-bit frontier town of Pearl Forks. For a man who, six months ago, had bet sixteen thousand dollars on the turn of a card in the finest gaming house in Eureka, falling this far was hard to accept.

Sebastian Ford still headed inside with a smile on his lips and fifty dollars in his pocket. Within the hour he'd doubled his stake in a poker game with two inebriated ranchers and a shifty-eyed mercantile owner, Brett Johnson.

After another hour, the betting became serious until he and Brett locked horns over what would surely be the last game of the session. While Sebastian sipped his whiskey, Brett leaned back in his chair and tapped his fingertips together.

As Sebastian had done six months

ago, they were playing five-card stud with two down and three up. Sebastian had three diamonds displayed while Brett had a run. Brett's lively gaze gave the impression he had a straight, which would win if Sebastian were bluffing about having a flush.

Trouble was, Sebastian *was* bluffing. But then again, he had won several bluffs that evening and his palms itched with a desire to try his luck again. The betting was with Sebastian and he bided his time, letting his opponent sweat and perhaps reveal more about himself.

'Come on,' Brett grumbled. 'You'll wear the cards out, staring at them like that.'

'Patience, my good friend,' Sebastian said. 'I'll take your money in my own time.'

The eliminated players chuckled while Sebastian fingered his bills and wondered whether he should risk resolving all his problems with this one hand.

Anticipation widened Brett's eyes, but then approaching footfalls sounded and Sebastian turned to see a newcomer crossing the saloon. He was trail-dirty and his jaw was set in a purposeful manner.

'Sebastian Ford?' he asked without preamble.

'Another delay!' Brett muttered with an exasperated sigh before Sebastian could decide whether to reply. 'This has to be the longest hand of poker I've ever played.'

Sebastian raised a hand to the newcomer and then shuffled forward to draw his belly up to the wood. The action hid the motion of him slipping a hand beneath the table.

'You want to hear my bet then, do you?' Sebastian said lightly.

Brett winced and then looked aloft before he nodded.

'Only for the last ten minutes.'

Sebastian smiled. He considered Brett while he listened to the newcomer walk around the table until he moved into his eye-line. The man's shadow crept across the table, making Brett turn and gesture at him to wait until they'd finished.

The man's face reddened, his intervention seemingly not playing out in the way he'd expected. Then he whirled his hand to his six-shooter.

Even before the gun had cleared leather, Sebastian pulled the trigger of his already drawn gun and blasted lead up through the table, slicing into the man's torso and making him drop.

The man landed on his chest. He strained his arms as he tried to raise himself, but he failed and he flopped down to lie still.

Sebastian glanced around the saloon, confirming that nobody else looked as if they were about to take exception to him. Then, with his free hand, he shoved everything he owned into the centre of the table, just as he had done on that ill-fated evening six months ago, albeit with a vastly higher stake.

'Can you match this?' he asked.

For almost a minute Brett stared at the dead man before, with a visible wrench, tearing his gaze away to consider the cards and then the pot. He rubbed his jaw nervously and glanced several times at the customers who were confirming the gunman's fate.

Sebastian sat back in his chair and holstered his gun. Then he tapped his fingertips together mimicking Brett's posture for the last few minutes as he reinforced his confidence.

'A dead man on the floor,' Brett said with a gulp, as if he'd decided to fold, 'and everything you own on the table. If ever I've met a man who doesn't bluff, it'd be you.'

Sebastian conceded his compliment with a nod. Then, with Brett saying nothing more, he moved to draw the pot back.

'Obliged,' he said.

His fingers were brushing the money when Brett shook his head. Then Brett pushed everything he had into the centre of the table and bellied up to the table in a mimic of Sebastian's earlier movement.

'The only problem is,' he said with a confident smile, 'I don't bluff either.'

Sebastian couldn't help but groan.

⋆   ⋆   ⋆

'I've checked out your story,' Sheriff McSween said. 'Everyone says that man came looking for trouble, that he drew first, and that he gave you no choice but to defend yourself.'

'Obliged,' Sebastian said with a relieved sigh. 'So can I go?'

'You can leave the law office.' McSween pointed to the door and then jerked his finger to the side to indicate the route along the main drag. 'Then keep on going and don't look back, even when you've left my town far behind.'

'But I've got no money, no horse, no nothing except for the clothes I'm wearing.'

'You've got a good pair of boots.

They'll cope with a few days afoot.' The sheriff slapped Sebastian's Peacemaker onto his desk. 'And as you've still got your gun, men like you will survive.'

'I'm no gunslinger,' Sebastian said, turning away.

While strapping on his holster, he headed to the door and was moving to walk outside when McSween coughed, halting him.

'Despite all the vivid descriptions I've heard of the events in the Pioneer Saloon, including the tale of a man losing two hundred dollars on a nothing hand, I've yet to hear the name of the dead man.'

Sebastian turned and considered the sheriff's raised eyebrows. Although his expression said that a name might make him soften his stance, Sebastian shrugged.

'I don't know it, but I've narrowed it down to five or six possibilities.'

Sebastian smiled, but his attempt at levity only made the sheriff scowl.

'You've got until sundown.' McSween

11

sat down and leaned back in his chair. 'If I don't have to run you out of town myself, when those other four or five come looking for you, I won't tell them which way you went.'

Sebastian tipped his hat and then left the office. Standing on the road, he considered the high sun, judging that he had five hours to leave town. As he didn't want to walk in the searing heat of the afternoon, he went in search of an alternative.

He couldn't find anybody who was planning to leave town today, although he did find Geoff White, the merchant who had taken pity on him and given him a ride to town. Unfortunately, Geoff reminded Sebastian that he still owed him the ten dollars he'd borrowed to make a fresh start in a new town.

Sebastian, promising to repay him tomorrow, then moved on. He'd used up most of the allotted time to McSween's deadline when he started wishing he'd taken the early walk instead.

He was being followed. He had thought he wouldn't encounter saloon owner Denver Fetterman as, during his three days in town, Denver hadn't ventured out of the Long Trail.

Sebastian walked briskly, keeping to the populated parts of town as he looked for a chance to run. Denver made no effort to move closer, an observation that delighted Sebastian until he saw the reason why.

Chuck Kelley, Denver's stalwart debt collector, was walking towards him, effectively trapping him. So Sebastian made a quick left into an alley that led only to a door twenty yards on.

He broke into a run, skidded to a halt by the door and shook it, but the door was bolted on the inside and, when he turned, Denver and Chuck were leaning nonchalantly against the corners of the alley.

'Nowhere to run,' Denver called.

Sebastian gave the door one last rattle. Then he walked to a point halfway down the alley where he stopped.

'I can't repay you yet,' he said. 'I have no money.'

'I'd heard that earlier you were betting heavily in the Pioneer Saloon.'

'Then you'll also have heard I lost heavily.' Sebastian settled his stance. 'And that I had some trouble.'

Denver smiled. 'I'd already gathered you were a man who made enemies quickly, which is why I want my two hundred dollars back now.'

'Two hundred!' Sebastian shook his head. 'I only borrowed fifty.'

Denver smirked. 'I hate complicated calculations, so my interest terms are simple. You borrowed fifty dollars and so the next day you owed me that money plus another fifty dollars. The next day — '

'I understand, but the thing is, I operate a simple system too, as the dead man in the Pioneer Saloon found out.'

Sebastian slapped a hand against his

holster, making both men scramble away. He wasn't a fast draw or an accurate shooter, but looking determined and acting quickly usually got him out of trouble without having to test either skill.

He waited for the men to show themselves, but when a minute passed without them reappearing, he checked he couldn't climb out of the cul-de-sac. Then, walking at a steady pace until he reached the end of the alley, he edged forward cautiously, expecting deception.

When it came, it was decisive.

Chuck and Denver had both pressed themselves flat to the wall. So, when he took a step out, Chuck leapt forward.

Chuck hammered two bunched hands down on the back of his neck, making him fold over, while in a co-ordinated move Denver kicked his feet from under him, depositing him on his chest. Then Chuck grabbed the back of his collar and hurled him back into the alley.

'As we're exchanging threats,' Denver said when Sebastian came to a halt lying on his side, 'I often have to explain to men like you the consequences of failing to repay debts. Unfortunately, Chuck usually has to tear them apart before they understand.'

Sebastian stood up. 'Come sunup I'll have your two hundred dollars.'

'I'm obliged, but make sure it's before sunup, because the moment the sun rises, you'll owe me two hundred and fifty dollars.' Denver waggled a finger at him. 'And don't leave town. If Chuck has to come looking for you, that'll only annoy him.'

Then, with smirks on their faces, the two men backed out of the alley.

This time Sebastian took his time in leaving. He batted the dust from his chest and knees and then shuffled to the corner.

He glanced out of the alley and confirmed that Denver and Chuck had gone. But that observation didn't cheer him.

Across the road, the sun was dipping down from view behind the buildings. Sundown would come in an hour.

2

Sundown found Sebastian complying with both Denver Fetterman's and Sheriff McSween's orders. He had left town, but for only fifty yards as he'd taken refuge behind the huge boulder that sat beside the town sign.

As he didn't relish the thought of walking through the night, he watched a group of ten covered wagons as they drew up outside town. They formed a line a quarter of a mile away, a distance far enough to suggest they liked their privacy.

Two men headed into town and emerged shortly afterwards laden down with supplies. The bustle that followed let Sebastian confirm that the wagon train had several families inside and that they weren't planning to move on today.

When their camp-fire was brighter

than the twilight redness on the horizon, Sebastian made his cautious way closer. He'd noted that the fifth wagon along the line was the least occupied. He had seen only a man and his son, presumably, of about sixteen use it.

This gave him hope that he might be able to sneak inside and then, if the owners slept outside tonight, remain undiscovered on the back of the wagon tomorrow until he'd gained some distance from town.

The firelight cast a glow on the ground for around a hundred yards; those around the fire busied themselves, intent on preparing a meal. Sebastian still skirted beyond the circle of light until he could move into the shadow of the first wagon. Then he hurried on to reach the back of the train where, in short bursts, he ran from wagon to wagon, pausing at each one.

He was preparing to run for the fourth time when grit crunched nearby. He froze, but a voice still spoke up.

'What are you doing there, mister?'

Sebastian put on a wide smile and then turned to find that a fresh-faced young man of around sixteen had discovered him. He reckoned he was probably the kid who used the wagon he was planning to sneak into.

'You folks looked like you might be friendly,' Sebastian said lightly, 'so I thought I'd introduce myself.'

'By sneaking around in the dark?'

Sebastian rubbed his jaw and, as he struggled to find an appropriate reply, a rangy man with a stern expression that the deep wrinkles said might be a permanent scowl came closer to stand at the kid's shoulder.

'What's the problem here, Gabriel?' he asked.

'I found this sneak thief, Pa. He was planning mischief.'

The man patted Gabriel's back and then moved into a defensive position between his son and Sebastian.

'I told Virgil we were wrong not to post guards. Towns like Pearl Forks are full of sneak thieves and good-for-nothing varmints. I'm pleased my son has more sense than our leader.'

With that last comment he'd raised his voice and, figuring it hadn't been made for his ears, Sebastian didn't retort.

Sure enough, a few moments later an authoritative-looking man with a trim beard joined them. He considered Sebastian with less distrust than the other two had and so Sebastian addressed his reply to him.

'I didn't mean to alarm you folks,' he said. 'I'd gathered in town that you weren't interested in mixing with the townsfolk, so I didn't know what kind of reception I'd get.'

'We avoid trouble,' Virgil said, 'but we're friendly with anyone who's friendly with us, so don't let Jeremiah's attitude make you think ill of us. Now, what do you want?'

While Jeremiah muttered something to himself, Sebastian took a deep breath and then provided the explanation he'd

21

worked out earlier in case he was discovered.

'I gather you folks are just passing through. Well, I've decided to move on too. I know the area and I know that plenty of good travellers such as yourselves have met with trouble.' He spread his hands. 'I offer my services as your guide for as long as I can help you.'

'We don't need no guide,' Jeremiah said. 'Especially one who sneaks around in the dark frightening kids.'

Jeremiah took Gabriel's shoulder and ushered him to back away, as if that were the final decision. Virgil considered them and then turned back to Sebastian.

'We're heading to Independence,' he said.

Sebastian flinched and he even put a hand to his brow as he thought quickly, his reaction being his first completely honest one since being discovered.

'I didn't know that,' he murmured. 'I thought you were heading west.'

'Is that a problem?' Virgil said. When Sebastian didn't reply, he continued. 'Is that an area you don't know?'

'I know Independence,' Sebastian said with a low tone before he brightened, figuring that anywhere was better than Pearl Forks. 'I was one of the first settlers there. I couldn't have been much older than Gabriel is now when we drew up and decided to stay. As it turned out, the area was a mighty fine place to live. We called it the land of lost dreams.'

Virgil considered his heartfelt speech and then turned to Jeremiah.

'We grouped together for protection through what could be a dangerous journey, and so a guide would be useful, provided his terms are reasonable.'

'I ask only,' Sebastian said when Jeremiah shook his head, 'to share your food while I share everything I know about your route ahead.'

Virgil nodded while Jeremiah walked up to Sebastian and looked him up and

23

down, his gaze lingering on his gun.

'Since I joined this wagon train our self-appointed leader has made some damn-fool decisions,' he said, 'so I'm not surprised he's made another one. We head on out at sunup. Be ready or we go without you.'

⋆ ⋆ ⋆

Sebastian judged that it was after midnight when he found a sheltered place to spend the rest of the night.

He'd figured that asking to stay with the wagon train during the night would raise suspicions about him not having belongings or a place to stay. So he'd returned to Pearl Forks where he'd done something he hadn't been desperate enough to do for years. He'd foraged.

By the light of the high moon, he'd worked his way along the backs of the buildings in town, picking up anything that had been discarded. He'd found half a coat and a heap of rags. His best find was a carpetbag that lacked a bottom and, when he'd found a coil of rope, he'd tied everything up in a bundle.

He judged that the pack was bulky enough to give the impression he was travelling light, provided nobody discovered what was inside. So, at the back of the stables, he rested his head on the bundle, spread the rags that were too threadbare to keep over his body and settled down for an uncomfortable night.

Despite his misgivings, his eyes closed quickly. Later, when a biting cold wind made him awake with a start, the moon had dipped down to the horizon.

He rooted around for the rags that must have blown away. When he couldn't find them he sat up and flinched again.

He had company. A large form was standing over him, holding up the rags at arm's length.

'Looking for these?' Chuck Kelley asked.

25

Sebastian didn't wait around for long enough to answer. He gained his feet quickly and moved away, but with his head down he ran into the dark shape of Denver Fetterman, who bundled him away.

Then, disorientated and in the dark, Sebastian struggled to gather his wits. So with ease, the two men combined forces to secure him.

He was disarmed and he had yet to get his breath back when he was thrown against the stable wall and treated to a low punch to the stomach that made him groan. Then he slid down the wall until he was in a seated position.

When it became clear he wasn't going to be hit again immediately, he cradled his stomach and took deep breaths until he'd regained enough strength to look up.

'Do you want to explain yourself?' Denver asked.

'I'll get your money for you,' Sebastian gasped.

Chuck slapped a heavy hand on his

shoulder and dragged him to his feet. He drew him forward and turned him round.

Then Chuck bent him double and ran him at the wall. He released him a pace from the wall not giving him enough time to throw his hands up to protect his face. He hammered into the wall headfirst with a heavy crunch.

His vision darkened and the next he knew he was lying on his back looking up at the dark outlines of Chuck and Denver, who were swimming in and out of focus.

'Second chance,' Denver said.

'I'm a gambler,' Sebastian murmured. 'It'll take time, but I'll — '

He didn't get to complete his excuse as Chuck stamped a boot on his belly and walked over him.

While Sebastian contented himself with a pained groan, Denver stood him upright. Then Chuck opened up his bundle of rags and slapped the carpetbag over his head and down to his shoulders so that his head was

27

pressed into a corner.

Chuck held his hands behind his back and then walked him along. With stinking rags pressed tightly against his face, Sebastian struggled even to breathe and so he let Chuck direct him while he concentrated on not stumbling.

They took him along the backs of the buildings and then through a door. With his hearing muffled too, Sebastian wasn't sure which building he'd been taken into, but he assumed it was the Long Trail.

He was led upstairs, down a corridor and to a room where he was pushed to his knees. The door closed and Chuck stood a pace behind him.

Several minutes passed before Chuck dragged the carpetbag off his head. Sebastian kept his head lowered until he'd got used to the bright light. Then he looked up at Denver Fetterman, who was now sitting at a desk.

'Third and final chance,' Denver said with a weary sigh, 'or this night will be the longest and final one of your life.'

'I don't know what you want.'

'You do.'

Chuck stomped forward and dragged Sebastian to his feet. Then from behind he thudded a low punch into his kidneys that made him stumble and then drop to his knees.

'All right,' Sebastian shouted before he could be hit again. 'I tried to leave town earlier.'

'Were you successful?'

Sebastian spread his hands and smiled. 'I'm still here, aren't I?'

'You are,' Denver said with a bored air that made cold dread clutch Sebastian's innards. 'Except you managed to ingratiate yourself with those settlers outside town. Apparently, you're now a reliable guide and at sunup you'll go with them, leaving your debt to me unpaid.'

'How do you know that?'

Denver waved a dismissive hand at him. 'I know everything that happens in my town.'

'Then why ask questions?'

Denver shrugged. 'So that Chuck can do what he does best.'

Sebastian winced. 'If I tell you that you've won and I've lost, will you stop toying with me and tell me what you want?'

Denver nodded and came out from behind his desk to stand before him.

'Many settlers pass through Pearl Forks. These days most of them reach their destination. Unfortunately, this latest group won't have a trouble-free journey. You'll direct them to head through the notorious Hangman's Gulch where some associates of mine led by Eleazer Fremont will waylay them.'

Sebastian's mouth fell open and although only one answer was required, he couldn't say it.

'They're dirt-poor settlers heading off in search of a new life because they have nothing in their old one. The pickings you'll get from them won't satisfy a man who owns the Long Trail.'

'That issue isn't your concern.'

Sebastian waited for a more detailed explanation, but when it didn't come, he uttered an exasperated sigh.

'And if I do this?'

'Your debt to me will be repaid. Heck, as I'm feeling generous, I'll even repay your debt to Geoff White. Best of all, you'll have a horse and a decent start on any other men who may come looking for you.'

Denver winked, confirming he knew Sebastian's troubles didn't end with him and so Sebastian adopted his best poker face and met Denver's eye.

'Hangman's Gulch is around five days away. Make sure Eleazer Fremont is waiting for us.'

'He'll be in position.' Denver waited until Sebastian got to his feet and then gestured at Chuck. 'And to make sure you don't feel an urge to lead them on a different route, Chuck will accompany you.'

Sebastian turned and considered Chuck's massive fists and his gap-toothed grin.

'Obliged,' he said.

31

3

'We hired you,' Virgil Michigan said, eyeing Chuck Kelley dubiously. 'I never said we needed anyone else.'

Sebastian had spent the last dregs of the night working out a revised story to explain Chuck's presence and so he had no difficulty in speaking with a light tone.

'Chuck also wants to leave Pearl Forks,' he said. He moved his horse closer to Virgil's wagon and leaned from the saddle to speak in a conspiratorial manner. 'And look at the size of him. Believe me, if we ride into trouble, you'll be glad he's with us.'

Virgil snorted a laugh and then beckoned for Sebastian and Chuck to ride up front. Sebastian followed his direction with a smile on his lips that changed to a frown when he'd moved out of Virgil's sight.

Although Denver Fetterman had given him a problem by demanding Chuck accompany him, he'd also helped his story sound more plausible by giving him a horse and a change of clothing. Now he didn't provide the impression that he'd had no choice but to leave town.

Even so, for the next few hours Sebastian glanced over his shoulder frequently, each time hoping that the sheriff hadn't noticed him sneaking out of town long after his deadline.

When he accepted he wasn't being followed, he settled into a steady riding rhythm and he let himself enjoy the simple pleasures of the wind on his face and the gradual change in the terrain. He tried to foster a feeling that he was riding away from his problems, but the thought kept returning that he was heading into a whole heap more.

As he and his unwelcome companion were supposed to know each other and they were riding at the front, he tried to exchange pleasantries, but Chuck

33

merely scowled at him until he gave up.

So, as they rode on through the morning, he considered the route ahead. For the first two days the journey would be a straightforward one so his role of guide wouldn't be needed. They would track along a wide valley in which the land gradually rose and the distant hills on either side became closer and steeper.

During the third day, they would veer into a narrower and winding valley that would lead to the sharp ridge known as the Devil's Hump. On the way up they would have several valleys to choose from and, with every change in direction, the choices would grow.

Some valleys led nowhere and others led to difficult routes over the ridge. Only one route would let them reach the most easily passable section of the Devil's Hump. That part of the journey would take two days, while a wrong turn would lead to them going back and forth for days until they found the right path.

After cresting the ridge, they would head down onto the gently sloping ground beyond that stretched ahead for another three days of travel to Independence.

If he carried out Denver's instructions, he wouldn't be guiding them along that final leg of the journey, as the journey down was a steep one and the most accessible route was through the notorious Hangman's Gulch.

Sebastian was determined that he wouldn't lead these people into an ambush and so he had four days to find a way to direct them to Independence using a different route.

That thought made him glance at Chuck and, almost as if he had picked up on his thoughts, his companion turned in the saddle to consider him. Chuck gave a slow shake of the head before he turned back to the front.

★   ★   ★

The evening found the settlers in good spirits.

35

During the day they had been quiet. Before now Sebastian had met only a few of the group, but with the day's travel complete everyone introduced themselves and then exchanged pleasantries before going back to their families.

As Chuck sat on his own and then rebuffed anyone who tried to talk to him, Sebastian made a point of being friendly. He hoped that by his own actions the surly Chuck might present him with a way out of his dilemma.

Later, Virgil and Temperance, the young woman he rode with, who Sebastian had discovered was his sister and not his wife, cooked a communal stew while the rest sat with their families in a circle around the fire. Then, when they'd collected their meal, everyone sat in informal groups.

Sebastian tried to join Virgil and Temperance's group, but it was already crowded, so he sat alone on the periphery until Gabriel joined him. The young man glanced at him several times until Sebastian shuffled closer.

'I'm sure,' Sebastian said, 'your pa wouldn't want you to sit with me.'

'I'm old enough to make my own decisions,' Gabriel said with a stern voice until he saw that Sebastian was smiling.

Gabriel returned the smile, although he then glanced around, presumably searching for his father. Jeremiah was eating with a group on the other side of the fire and not looking their way. So he leaned towards him and asked the question Sebastian had been anticipating.

'What's Independence like?'

'It's a good place to settle down. You folk chose well and the people there will welcome you.'

Gabriel frowned. 'If Independence is that good, why did you leave?'

'Because it was too good for me.' Sebastian's comment made Gabriel furrow his brow and so he continued. 'I have a knack of using up a place. I get involved in more things than are

37

healthy for me and before long I need to move on.'

Gabriel looked away and chewed thoughtfully for a while.

'I understand,' he said with a wistful tone that suggested that, despite his youth, he knew the problem. 'Last night you said you were about my age when you stopped there.'

'I was, and I stayed for five years.'

Gabriel sighed. 'I don't reckon I'll stay that long. This is a big country and Independence sounds like a small place.'

'Your family will miss you.'

'I've only got my pa now,' Gabriel snapped, an angry high-pitched lilt replacing his former light tone. 'My mother's no longer with us.'

Sebastian provided an understanding frown. 'When did she die?'

'She didn't,' Gabriel said, his tone terse. 'She left us. She didn't want to join Virgil's wagon train. Pa ignored her and, when we reached Eureka, they had another argument. She ran away. Pa can do that to you.'

'He's a stern man, but he's doing the best he can.'

'He isn't. Since she left, he's been angry all the time.'

Gabriel threw his plate to the ground with the last of his food uneaten.

'And not just him, I see.'

'How do you expect me to behave?' Gabriel said, rounding on him. 'She left me with him, so she doesn't care about me, and neither does he.'

'I understand what you're going through.' Sebastian picked up Gabriel's plate and held it out. 'Except I never got the chance to put things right. Both my mother and my father died on the way to the land of lost dreams.'

Gabriel's shoulders sagged and he snatched the plate from Sebastian's grasp. Then he poked at his food until, finally, he gave Sebastian a brief nod of thanks.

'Why did you call it that — the land of lost dreams?' he said after a while.

'For the people like my parents who died on the way; for the others who died in the first harsh winter; for the next band of settlers who were killed by raiders in Hangman's Gulch. All those people never got to enjoy their dream of a new life in a new land.'

'Did you catch the raiders?' Gabriel asked with a nervous gulp and a glance around, as if these men might still be about.

'The townsfolk banded together and tracked them down. They delivered summary justice in the gulch. Then they left the bodies dangling at the entrance as a warning. It must have worked, as no dreams have been lost since.'

Gabriel opened his mouth, but before he could speak, his father arrived. Jeremiah pointed at his son and then jerked his finger over his shoulder. Without comment, Gabriel scurried away.

'What were you talking about?' Jeremiah demanded with his hands on his hips.

'About recent events.' Sebastian

coughed. 'I'm sorry to hear about what happened with your wife.'

'That's not got nothing to do with you,' Jeremiah snapped, his eyes blazing in the firelight.

'It hasn't.'

Jeremiah continued to glare at him until he acknowledged his acquiescence with a stern nod.

'So keep away from Gabriel. He doesn't need a man like you filling his head with nonsense at a time like this.'

Sebastian shrugged. 'Gabriel seems a smart and sensible young man who's old enough to pick his own friends and make his own decisions.'

'Not yet he isn't. He still . . . ' Jeremiah trailed off and glanced aside to see that their conversation had gathered the interest of several others, although everyone then looked away.

'All right,' Sebastian said with a low voice. 'You're Gabriel's father and you have the right to tell me not to speak to him again, but I hope that one day I'll earn your respect. Until then, I'll do your bidding.'

Jeremiah firmed his jaw as he seemingly considered this statement for hidden traps. Then he gave a brief nod and turned away to follow Gabriel back to their wagon, leaving Sebastian to eat the last of his meal in thoughtful silence.

When he'd finished, he handed in his plate to Temperance and, as he'd noticed that Chuck had said nothing, he expressed his thanks and praised the meal. Then he looked for Chuck, finding him walking away from the camp.

Adopting a casual pace and posture, Sebastian followed him at a distance, but when he'd moved beyond the circle of firelight, it became hard to keep his footing in the brush and he stumbled several times. Before long, he'd lost sight of his quarry.

Worried that Chuck had a malicious intent such as signalling to Eleazer Fremont, he followed Chuck's last direction. He'd covered a hundred yards when a voice spoke up from the dark.

'That Jeremiah Riddle spoke a lot of sense,' Chuck said. 'Stay away from the kid, and everyone else.'

'We're guests of these folk,' Sebastian said, 'and so I'm being friendly, or else come the day that I tell them to head down through Hangman's Gulch, they're likely to ignore me.'

'Your role is to guide them. My role is to watch you.' Chuck emerged from out of the darkness to loom over him, his form several feet taller than usual. 'Which is what I'm doing.'

Sebastian had just worked out that Chuck was standing on a rock when he leapt from it. With his hands thrown up, Chuck grabbed Sebastian's shoulders and knocked him over onto his back.

Sebastian went down heavily with Chuck flattening him to the ground. He tried to buck him, but he was winded and Chuck was too heavy.

So he just lay there until Chuck

levered himself off him. Then he moved to roll aside, but he couldn't escape Chuck's clutches and a massive hand slapped down on his shoulder, halting him.

Firm slaps to the cheeks rocked his head from side to side and then a chop into the stomach made him sit up, gagging. He was still struggling to avoid retching his meal back up when Chuck drew him to his feet.

With one hand wrapped around his throat, Chuck raised him onto his tiptoes.

'Get off me,' Sebastian gasped.

'I don't follow your orders,' Chuck muttered. 'And I don't believe your lies. I know you're trying to make friends and gather allies to take me on. So stop the scheming. These people are walking dead men and you will be too if you defy Denver.'

Sebastian tried to reply, but when his voice emerged as a strangulated squeak Chuck relaxed his grip and let him drop back down onto his heels.

'That's the longest speech I've ever heard you make,' Sebastian said. 'That means you're scared.'

Chuck erupted with a snorting boom of laughter.

'Me? Scared?'

'Yeah, because if you don't follow your orders, you're a walking dead man too.'

'I sure am,' Chuck said, lowering his voice. 'But all you need to think about is: if I fail, I'll spend my last hours making you beg to die.'

With a grunt of triumph Chuck thrust his arm straight up to hold Sebastian off the ground. For a seeming eternity motes of light danced before Sebastian's eyes and blood pounded in his ears until Chuck threw him aside.

He landed on his side, choking and gasping in air, but Chuck hadn't finished with him yet. He hunkered down beside him, his shape a huge absence of light in the dark.

'And all you need to think about,' Sebastian said between gasps, 'is that for the next few days I have the advantage. You can't kill me because without me, the settlers will go where they please.'

Chuck snorted his breath through his nostrils. Then he slapped the side of Sebastian's head with the back of his hand, sending him tumbling away to land face first in the dirt.

As he lay there, Sebastian sensed Chuck moving along to stand over him, but he couldn't summon the strength to defend himself.

'The moment you disobey Denver,' Chuck muttered, 'I'll start shooting your settler friends. I'll make sure I get that kid you like first.'

Chuck tapped a foot against his hip, but Sebastian didn't want to risk prolonging the fight with another retort. Presently, Chuck stopped kicking him and, when Sebastian heard footfalls pacing away, he rolled onto his side to gasp in air.

After a few minutes, the bone-aching coldness of the ground forced him to get up. He faced the camp; between him and the firelight stood a man's form.

Unbidden, Sebastian backed away for a pace until he noticed that the man was too small to be Chuck.

He moved closer, his steps uncertain at first until he gathered his wits about him. Then he recognized Virgil; he was looking directly at him.

How much he'd heard and seen of what had just happened Sebastian couldn't tell, and so he hailed him with a cheery wave.

Virgil said nothing until he joined him where he moved so that both men could see each other in the firelight. For several seconds Virgil appraised him and when he spoke his tone was determined.

'Who are you?' he asked. 'And what do you want?'

4

'As I told you,' Sebastian said, 'I'm Sebastian Ford and I want to guide you to Independence, a town I know well.'

'Who is your friend?' Virgil said after a while. 'And what does he want?'

'As I'm sure you've worked out, Chuck's no friend of mine, but he has his own reasons for joining this expedition. You should ask him what they are.'

'I will,' Virgil said, his tone becoming lighter suggesting he hadn't seen the entire incident in the brush. 'But right now I'm asking *you*; why were you so keen to leave Pearl Forks?'

'I got into some trouble after a poker game.' Sebastian waited, but Virgil didn't reply and so he continued. 'I had to kill a man who came looking for me in the Pioneer Saloon.'

Virgil gave an affirmative grunt. 'I

heard about that incident when we bought supplies and I've wondered if that man was you. Now you've admitted to that, what about the rest?'

'Others have a problem with me and they're sure to come after me, but I'm the only one in danger.'

'And why are they interested in you?'

'I can't say.' Sebastian shrugged when Virgil rocked from foot to foot in irritation. 'Answering that would put you in danger.'

'I'll take that risk.'

Sebastian rubbed his hands together and then pointed at the fire. Virgil nodded and so the two men headed back to the camp where they sat down in a warm area, far enough away from everyone to keep their conversation private.

When the fire had eased the soreness from the beating Chuck had administered, Sebastian took a deep breath.

'Six months ago I got into the biggest poker game of my life in Eureka.'

'We passed through that town. It

looked impressive.' Virgil sighed. 'One of our group even decided to stay.'

'I'd heard, and that place had the same effect on me. I felt so confident I talked myself into a game with Dawson Breen, the owner of the Bonanza House and the most powerful man in town. Sixteen thousand dollars were on the table and their destination hinged on the turn of a single card.'

'You don't look like a man who's got even sixteen cents to his name, so I'd guess that card turned bad?'

Sebastian shook his head. 'It was worse. I won. The only problem was, I then had to cash in my chips and that wasn't sensible in a town Dawson owned.'

'What did you do?'

'As I'd effectively played the house, the house rule was that all debts or payments had to be settled within one year. As I figured I'd be killed when I left the gaming house with my money, I sneaked away. I'd planned to return with protection, but I've spent the last six months running with Dawson's men at my heels.'

'Do you still plan to return?'

Sebastian couldn't help but laugh. 'That would be certain death. Eureka will have to remain *my* land of lost dreams.'

Virgil rubbed his jaw and then nodded. 'I believe your story, but I find it interesting that after six months of running, you haven't moved further away. We passed through Eureka two weeks ago.'

As Sebastian had no answer to this, he could only smile.

★ ★ ★

Despite the ominous feeling the fight with Chuck had given Sebastian, the second day of travelling passed peacefully.

As before, he rode at the front with Chuck, who made no effort to be friendlier than he had been on the first day, but neither was he more antagonistic. Sebastian looked out for Virgil questioning him, but he didn't see them talking.

They made good time and at sundown, the wagon train reached the valley from where they would veer away to the north.

They settled down for the night, and Sebastian enjoyed a sociable evening, exchanging friendly chatter with anyone who approached him, and he did as he'd been asked by avoiding Jeremiah and Gabriel. Chuck ignored him along with everyone else.

On the third day, they set off for the distant ridge that around noon became visible as a faint, lighter patch against the sky. When he was sure about what he could see ahead, Sebastian bade everyone to stop. The wagons spread out on either side of him to form a line and consider the task they faced.

'Which way?' someone called.

Sebastian turned to the speaker. He took a moment to reply as only then did he see that Jeremiah had spoken, his voice less truculent than the last time they'd talked. At his side, Gabriel was making a show of not looking at him.

'We follow this valley until mid-afternoon.' He pointed east. 'Then we veer away, always turning to the left until we climb up the side of a bluff to a ridge. The next day we track along high ground and by sundown we'll reach the base of the Devil's Hump where we can rest up for the long day ahead.'

'If you're right about that,' said Jeremiah, 'we can't waste time standing around here talking all day.'

Sebastian couldn't disagree with that and he moved off, but as the day wore on, doubts assailed him that his schedule was right. Until now his main concern had been working out how he could avoid Eleazer Fremont without incurring Chuck's wrath.

Now practical concerns occupied his thoughts. It'd been seven years since he'd last traversed the area and he found that his memory wasn't as good as he'd hoped it would be.

He didn't notice as many landmarks

as he expected. Worse, he knew the route from hunting expeditions. Back then he'd travelled alone or in small groups that moved quickly, so when he did see familiar points that confirmed he was on the right path, they came slower than expected.

With lumbering wagons trailing behind him, the distant Devil's Hump stayed as just a light patch on the horizon and the closer ridge failed to appear. He kept expecting it to appear beyond the next bend or when they'd passed the next high point that blocked their view, but it remained unseen.

So it was with some relief that the ridge finally appeared to his left, emerging from behind a precipitous peak. But by now the sun was dipping down towards the bluff, giving him a new doubt as to whether they would reach the position he'd hoped to reach by sundown.

He kept that thought to himself and continued to seek out the route that took them around the bluff. When he found it, the sun had dropped from view and he judged that they had only an hour to accomplish a journey that he had expected would take most of the afternoon.

As a thin dribble of a creek meandered down towards them, signalling that they were on the last flat ground for a while, he beckoned Virgil to join him and, after a brief consultation, Virgil called a halt for the day. The reaction was as he'd expected.

Everyone was pleased the day's journey was over and nobody mentioned his prediction about their progress, although Jeremiah swung his wagon by. He looked from Sebastian to the Devil's Hump and back again with a significant glance that confirmed he hadn't forgotten.

Chuck also sidled closer; he stared at the bluff and then beyond at the nearest ridge.

'We'll struggle to reach the Devil's Hump in time,' he said.

'Sure,' Sebastian said with a smile.

'But then again, I'm in no hurry.'

Then he moved away before Chuck could retort. For the next hour, he always stayed close to someone so there could be no repeat of the first night's unpleasantness. When his steady wandering took him to Virgil, he was drawn aside.

'Jeremiah's complained again about me not posting guards,' he said. 'I didn't think it necessary before, but what would you advise now?'

'This is a dangerous area,' Sebastian said, feeling pleased that Virgil had given him a natural opportunity to lay the seeds for raising concern about their proposed route later. 'Settlers have been raided around here before.'

'I asked in each town we passed through and I gather that was years ago. Nobody had heard about trouble recently.'

'That's true, but we wouldn't want to prove them wrong.'

'We wouldn't.' Virgil spread his hands. 'But look at us. We have nothing anyone would want to raid.'

Sebastian frowned; this was the other issue that had never been far from his thoughts. Why was Denver Fetterman going to so much trouble to waylay these people when they had nothing worth stealing?

'To people who have nothing,' he ventured, 'you have everything.'

Virgil glanced up at the route they'd have to take tomorrow and then nodded.

'I understand. I'll tell Jeremiah I support his idea. That might make him more sociable.'

When Virgil left him, Sebastian's more relaxed mood didn't last for long as, after hearing the news, he was the first person Jeremiah sought out.

'I'm posting guards through the night,' Jeremiah said. 'You're with me for the first watch.'

Jeremiah then set off uphill, walking purposefully. On the other side of the camp, Virgil caught his eye and winked, making Sebastian snort a laugh before he followed him.

Jeremiah set a brisk pace until he reached a ledge that overlooked the camp. He looked back along the route they'd taken. Then he looked up at the route they'd take, his intense gaze seeming to memorize every rock and bush.

'This,' Sebastian said when Jeremiah had finished, 'is the ideal place to keep lookout.'

'I know,' Jeremiah said. 'That's why I chose it. This time we should be able to see any unwanted newcomers sneaking up on the camp.'

Jeremiah turned to him for the first time, but Sebastian ignored the bait and took the comment at face value.

'It'll be easy to do that tonight, but it'll get harder when the terrain closes in and we have to travel through areas that are overlooked by high rocks on either side.'

Jeremiah nodded and then moved away for a few paces. When he settled down, lying on his front and looking at the camp, Sebastian sat up and looked in the opposite direction.

For the next hour, as the light level dropped, neither man spoke, although Sebastian continued to feel uncomfortable in Jeremiah's company. So when he glimpsed a glow out of the corner of his eye, perhaps from reflected light, on a ledge two hundred feet away, he balked at the possibility of annoying him if he was wrong.

Only when the light flashed again did he put aside his misgivings and draw Jeremiah closer.

'What do you make of that?' he asked, pointing up the side of the bluff.

Jeremiah joined him and narrowed his eyes.

'I don't see nothing,' he said after a while.

'I thought I saw something flash up there.'

'A signal?'

'Could be.'

Jeremiah slapped his shoulder and then moved off quickly. He didn't ask for directions and, with his head down, he scurried from rock to rock with the ease of a man who knew what he was doing.

Sebastian stayed ten feet behind him, following the same route and, with unerring accuracy, Jeremiah headed to the right area. Only when he was twenty feet below the ledge did he stop and take refuge behind a boulder.

When Sebastian joined him, with hand signals alone Jeremiah directed him to move up to the right of the ledge while he took a left-hand path that would bring him out above it. Sebastian nodded and, matching Jeremiah's cautious behaviour, he kept low while looking out for any movement.

He saw nothing and, for that matter, other than the two earlier flashes, he'd seen nothing untoward since. When he reached a point where he would be able to see what was on the ledge if he stood upright, he waited for Jeremiah to get into position.

A few moments later Jeremiah

appeared at his destination. He glanced at the ledge and then dropped down from view with a speed that told Sebastian he hadn't been wrong about seeing something up here. Sebastian also dropped down to lie flat where he waited, his gun aimed at the edge of the rock.

Presently, Jeremiah appeared again. He risked another quick glance. Then he took a longer look before, with a raised hand, he beckoned Sebastian to stay where he was while he moved in.

At first, Jeremiah inched forward, but when he'd moved to a few paces from the ledge, he straightened and speeded. Then he jumped down onto the ledge and disappeared from view.

Scuffing footfalls sounded before he looked over the edge with his upper lip curled in disgust.

'Bodies,' he said simply.

Sebastian provided an appropriately concerned look and then clambered up to join him. A man lay on his side facing the edge while behind him lay a woman.

Sebastian stayed back while Jeremiah shuffled closer. He was leaning forward to examine the bodies when he flinched and backed away, his gun swinging up to aim at the woman, who, to Sebastian's surprise, raised a hand in which she held a lawman's star.

'You saw me,' she croaked before flopping over onto her back.

Sebastian hurried in while this time Jeremiah stayed back. Sebastian confirmed that the lawman was dead, but when he moved to help the woman, he also flinched, now realizing what had concerned Jeremiah.

The woman was manacled to the dead lawman.

5

The woman's name was Amelia Cook and the dead man had been US Marshal Jack Aldiss. She was too exhausted and distressed to provide more details.

So Sebastian and Jeremiah concentrated on getting her down to the wagons. This proved to be difficult, as the dead man was heavy and the incline steep.

Thankfully, after they'd struggled to move her a few dozen yards, the burly Clement Wainwright, a man Virgil often conferred with, arrived from the camp. Sebastian explained the problem and Clement brought up two boards to use as makeshift stretchers.

Once they were in the camp, Amelia gratefully accepted water. Apparently, the key to the handcuffs had been lost but Clement had a plan. He fetched a pick and then splayed out her chain to its maximum extent. With her face averted, he required only one accurate blow to open the manacle around the dead marshal's wrist.

When Amelia was moved away from the body, she brightened. Although she glanced at the manacle around her own wrist frequently, Clement didn't attempt to remove it.

Then she was left alone with only Temperance standing unobtrusive guard over her.

For the next thirty minutes everyone returned to the normal routine for the evening and, with Amelia no longer being the centre of attention, she relaxed enough to indicate that she felt well enough to talk.

'Marshal Aldiss died last night,' she said when Virgil, Jeremiah and Sebastian had gathered around her. 'So I've spent today steeling myself to get free. It wouldn't have been nice.'

'But better than dying chained to a dead man,' Virgil said. He looked around with a benign expression, but when nobody had anything soothing to say, he asked one of the obvious questions. 'How did he die?'

She felt the manacle that was still around her wrist.

'We were attacked coming down from the ridge by about ten men. We fell.' She pointed upwards, indicating a point on the bluff, although it was now too dark for her to find the exact spot. 'They stole our horses and left us for dead.'

'Do you know who they were?'

'No. They just came out of nowhere. The marshal didn't have a chance.' She rattled her manacle. 'But you have nothing to fear from me. This isn't what it seems.'

'I'm sure it isn't.' Virgil offered a smile. 'But we'll let the authorities in Independence decide that.'

She opened her mouth to reply, but then thought better of it and provided an unconcerned shrug while looking at the cooking pot.

As the evening meal was now ready, Virgil relented from the questioning. He beckoned Temperance to bring Amelia a plate and tasked Clement with guarding her.

'You do know,' Sebastian said when he, Jeremiah and Virgil had moved out of her hearing range, 'that there are no authorities in Independence, don't you? The folk there sort out their own problems; they don't have time for other people's issues.'

Jeremiah cast Virgil an aggrieved glare before Virgil replied.

'I know that,' he said lightly. 'I wanted to know if she knew, and I'd judge from her attempt to appear unconcerned that she's been to Independence. She might even have done whatever got her arrested there.'

With that comment, Virgil rose, delivering instructions for guard duty for the remainder of the night before he left.

'If he keeps this up,' Jeremiah said, nodding approvingly as he watched

Virgil go, 'he might make a leader, after all.'

Sebastian nodded and then, with Jeremiah having made what was probably his first non-aggressive comment to him, he gestured at the woman.

'What do you make of her?' he asked.

'Trouble, in the past, present and future.'

'So what would you do with her, if you were in charge?'

Jeremiah rubbed his jaw and Sebastian reckoned that his furrowed brow meant he was about to provide an unacceptable solution, but with the dishing out of the meal getting underway, Gabriel was coming closer and so he just shrugged.

'I'd let her go. It'd be easier.'

If that was his real preferred solution, he didn't express it again when, later that night, Virgil called a meeting.

Firstly, Virgil ordered Amelia to be secured to a wagon wheel using rope attached to the manacle. Then he left Temperance watching over her and went to stand by the fire in the middle of the circle of settlers where he asked for opinions about her and about the journey ahead.

The subsequent debate was stilted, probably because she was close enough to hear them, and nobody argued when Virgil stated his plan to keep her secured until they reached Independence. But the latter element of this plan did generate debate.

Nobody was against continuing on to Independence, but knowing that raiders were ahead worried everyone. The settlers wanted more details of what lay ahead and so Amelia was escorted into the circle.

In a faltering voice she told them everything she knew about the men who had attacked her and about the marshal, although that wasn't much more than what she'd said earlier.

While she spoke, Sebastian glanced at Chuck. As nobody was watching him, Chuck met his gaze and smiled. Then he looked up at the dark mass of the Devil's Hump and mimed a knife cut across his throat.

★ ★ ★

Despite Sebastian's misgivings, the next morning the main problem everyone faced was the tougher terrain.

Virgil stationed guards to follow on behind the wagon train while Sebastian and Chuck went on ahead. Sebastian didn't ask Chuck what he thought about Amelia's unexpected arrival, as he doubted he'd be helpful.

What was clear was that Eleazer Fremont had passed this way, leaving no doubt that he would carry out Denver's plan. When, in the early afternoon, they crested the first ridge and the Devil's Hump came into full view, the problems Sebastian faced felt imminent.

The ridge appeared to be so close he could reach out and touch it, although he was sure they wouldn't crest it for at least two days. Chuck had the same concern and while they waited for the wagons to catch up with them, he glared at the ridge and then at Sebastian.

'We were supposed to head down from the ridge tomorrow,' he muttered. 'But we're sure to be a day late now.'

'That means,' Sebastian said with an unconcerned tone, 'that Eleazer will just have to wait for a little longer.'

Chuck grunted with irritation and then treated him to a barrage of abuse and threats, giving vent to a frustration that he'd clearly been storing up for a while. Sebastian let him have his say.

Chuck didn't relent until the first wagons were closing on them. When he moved on, Sebastian noted that Virgil was in the lead wagon. Virgil gave him a bemused shrug, questioning what the argument had been about, and Sebastian responded with a shrug of his own.

When he followed Chuck, he did so with a smile on his lips. Although he was unsure if he should risk telling Virgil the full story, Chuck's surly behaviour had laid the groundwork for him to speak with Virgil about his problem.

Throughout the afternoon he kept his good humour even when the journey across the high ground was slower than he expected. Stretches of loose rock made the going tough for the wagon wheels and Sebastian judged they'd covered only a quarter of the way to the base of the Devil's Hump when Virgil called everyone to a halt.

He chose an exposed spot that promised a cold night, but which also made it hard for anyone to sneak up on them. He stationed men ahead and behind and, as with last night, he and Jeremiah took the first watch.

This time they encountered no problems on their watch, not that Sebastian expected any, and he used the time to think through the remainder of the journey. He judged that by tomorrow night they'd have reached the base of the Devil's Hump.

With them making the journey up and then down on the next day, they would arrive later than expected, but this gave Sebastian more time to speak with Virgil privately. So, when he returned to the camp, he acted calmly and waited for a natural meeting that wouldn't make Chuck suspicious.

As it was, Chuck already appeared on edge and he even ate in the circle for the first time. That had the unfortunate effect of making Virgil notice him and he allocated him the duty of keeping the last watch of the night. Chuck accepted the order with a muttered oath while Sebastian decided he'd talk with Virgil then.

When Sebastian had collected his meal, Gabriel sat with him. While he ate, Gabriel said nothing, but he did cast frequent glances around the camp.

Sebastian thought he was checking whether his father had noticed he was sitting beside him. But after studying

Gabriel, he worked out he was looking at Amelia, who was again tied to a wagon wheel.

'Pa says,' Gabriel said after a while, 'that he doesn't mind if you and I speak now.'

'I'm pleased,' Sebastian said, 'that I've earned his respect.'

Gabriel smiled. 'You haven't. He told me to listen to everything you say and then to do the opposite.'

Sebastian laughed. 'That's good advice.'

Gabriel shrugged and kicked at the stones around his feet. He again looked at Amelia, but this time he noticed that Sebastian was looking at him and so he sighed.

'She's an amazing woman, isn't she?' he asked wistfully.

'I've only said a few words to her, so I'm not sure yet.'

'But you don't need to speak with her to know she's not like any other woman you've ever met.' Gabriel frowned. 'Although you probably have

73

met other women like her.'

'I have, although only when armed and after I'd hidden my money.' Sebastian leaned closer to him and lowered his voice. 'I know your father wants you to do the opposite of everything I say, but with Amelia, stop thinking about her and think about women your own age.'

Gabriel pointed around the circle of settlers.

'There aren't any women my own age here and it doesn't sound as if they'll be any in Independence either.'

As he was probably right, Sebastian couldn't think of an appropriate reply and so they sat in silence for a while.

Gabriel didn't take his advice, however, and continued to glance often at Amelia. Later, with even the roaring fire struggling to keep the cold at bay, everyone headed quickly to their wagons.

As on previous nights, Sebastian settled down close to the fire. Chuck picked a spot on the opposite side of the flames, he being the only person other than the guards and Amelia who was outside.

With Chuck being restless and Sebastian finding it hard to sleep with so much on his mind, he wandered over to Amelia, who was swaddled in a nest of blankets.

She acknowledged him with a warm smile, but other than confirming that she was comfortable, she wasn't interested in conversation.

Sebastian returned to the fire where another hour passed before he fell into a fitful sleep. But his determination to ensure that he awoke when Chuck left for his guard duty didn't let him rest fully.

So when footfalls approached, he became quickly alert and was already starting to sit up when Jeremiah shook his shoulder.

'What's wrong?' Sebastian asked.

'Gabriel's gone,' Jeremiah said, his eyes bright in the firelight and his tone accusing.

'Perhaps he's on guard duty.'

'His session ended earlier, except he didn't come back afterwards.' Jeremiah pointed across the campsite at a tangle of blankets. 'And worse, Amelia's gone too.'

6

When the settlers had all been woken up and compared stories, the situation was no clearer other than the basic facts that Gabriel and Amelia were no longer in the camp.

Jeremiah stalked around, barking out questions and glaring towards the east as if by the force of his stare he could encourage the sun to rise so they could begin searching for his son. Only when it was discovered that supplies had gone missing did his fears about foul play recede.

'That means it's unlikely they were both kidnapped,' Jeremiah said. 'But did he take her? Or did she take him?'

With nobody being prepared to answer, Sebastian spoke up.

'Last night Gabriel seemed to be fascinated by her,' he said. 'So I'd guess that while he was on guard duty he talked with her, and then . . . and then something happened.'

'Such as?'

Sebastian waved his arms, but with Jeremiah's furious gaze boring into him, he felt he had no choice but to answer, albeit phrased using a positive version of events.

'She encouraged him,' he said. 'That made him feel sorry for her. So he freed her.'

'But why would he then leave with her?'

Sebastian reckoned his brief conversation with Gabriel provided an obvious reason, but he didn't think Jeremiah would appreciate the suggestion that Gabriel was besotted with her, so he shrugged.

'Perhaps he didn't want to disappoint you.'

'Then he failed,' Jeremiah muttered and he began stalking back and forth. 'And so have you. I knew letting him talk to you was a mistake. You did what I feared you would and fired him up with tales about your exploits.'

Jeremiah set his hands on his hips, defying Sebastian to disagree.

'I told him to put her out of his mind, but obviously telling a young man that was doomed to fail.'

Jeremiah frowned, clearly unwilling to admit Sebastian was right, but also lost for anything to say until he bunched a fist.

'What can a woman and a kid hope to do out there afoot?'

'With raiders about they'll have to be cautious,' Virgil said, joining in the debate for the first time, presumably to save Sebastian from annoying Jeremiah again by replying. 'So they won't have gone far.'

'That means we don't have to wait for the light,' Jeremiah said, slapping a fist into his palm. He turned to the south. 'My son's no fool. He'll have directed her away from any trouble and back towards Pearl Forks.'

'You could easily ride by them in the dark,' Virgil said. 'Gabriel won't have come to harm yet, so wait and we'll organize a proper search in the morning.'

Jeremiah shot another glance at the thin stream of light on the eastern horizon and then gave a curt nod before heading back to his wagon, effectively postponing the other debate of who would be in the search party.

'I'll send Clement Wainwright with him,' Virgil said, joining Sebastian. 'The rest of us will carry on to Independence, and Jeremiah and Clement can follow on behind when they've found Gabriel.'

'They'll need to be careful too,' Sebastian said.

'Travelling light, they'll find it easier to avoid the raiders than we will.' Virgil slapped a hand on his shoulder. 'Which means you need to stop worrying about them and concentrate on keeping us safe.'

★　★　★

Sun up found Chuck in good spirits for the first time that Sebastian had seen and Sebastian's gloomy demeanour only went to delight him even more.

'Don't look so annoyed,' Chuck declared as they rode along a quarter-mile on from the wagon train. 'That kid's made things easy for you. Everyone's too concerned about what happened to Gabriel to look out for Eleazer.'

Chuck leered at him, seemingly defying him to admit that this turn of events was bad news.

'They are,' Sebastian said, meeting Chuck's gaze. 'But plenty can happen between now and tomorrow when we head down into Hangman's Gulch. Let's hope Eleazer doesn't get bored and move on.'

This comment did at least remove Chuck's smirk, letting them ride along in silence so that Sebastian could reconsider how he would defy Denver's orders. Chuck appeared aware of his thoughts as, unlike on the previous days, he stayed close to him, not giving him a chance to confide in Virgil.

As the day wore on, the gradually rising land let them see back along their route for many miles, but there was no sign of anyone following on behind.

They had yet to catch sight of Jeremiah and Clement when, that night, they stopped at the base of the final climb up to the Devil's Hump. Sebastian spoke quietly with Virgil. Then Virgil explained to everyone that tomorrow they would need to set off at first light to ensure they could crest the summit and reach the flatter ground on the other side in one day.

As Chuck had now become his shadow, Sebastian didn't mention the possibility of them using an alternate route, although he chose his words carefully by avoiding mentioning Hangman's Gulch.

After a long day, the settlers were exhausted and their spirits were low. They dropped even lower when Clement joined them, sporting an aggrieved expression and a livid bruise on his cheek. Apparently he and Jeremiah had disagreed about the best way to search for Gabriel and the result had been a parting of the ways.

After this unsurprising revelation, Virgil didn't post any guards that night. He explained that in such an exposed place nobody would be able to approach them silently. Sebastian didn't disagree, as trouble would be waiting for them on the other side of the ridge anyway.

When they set off the next morning, Jeremiah still hadn't returned. By the time they'd traversed half of the way up to the summit of the ridge, the clear air and the high point let the settlers see for many miles and confirm that he and Gabriel wouldn't be joining them.

With that matter now resolved, Sebastian put his mind to the task ahead. The settlers were straggled out below and so he stayed close to Virgil in the lead wagon in the hope that Chuck would move on ahead.

Chuck responded by riding between Sebastian and Virgil's wagon, giving him no chance of having a private conversation. When they reached the top, the train had spread out in a line below. Virgil drew to a halt.

Sebastian dismounted and found a sharp stone and a patch of loose dirt. By the time Virgil jumped down and joined him, he had sketched out a map of the area.

Chuck moved his horse to stand over him while he glared down at the map as if it might contain hidden traps, but when Sebastian pointed at Hangman's Gulch, he grunted with approval. Then he moved to circle around them, but struggled to control his mount over a patch of rough stones and his horse edged sideways, scattering Sebastian and Virgil.

When they'd righted themselves, hoofs had obliterated the map, making Temperance lean out of the wagon and glare at him.

'Why did you do that?' she demanded.

'He needs to understand the route.'

Chuck sneered, seemingly unwilling to offer an apology for his mistake. Instead, he moved his horse round to her side. While he gave Temperance a surly reply, Sebastian sketched the map again quickly.

'This route is our first option for going down,' he said, pointing.

'Obliged for that, but why is he so edgy?' Virgil said, as an argument developed between Temperance and Chuck.

'He has good reason.' Sebastian's urgent tone made Virgil turn back. Then he pointed at a treacherous unnamed route down two miles on. 'You'll ignore the first option and go down through the second one.'

'I understand,' Virgil said, now looking at the map carefully, 'but if we get into difficulties, we'll just follow you and Chuck.'

'You won't. Chuck and I have agreed that we'll scout around on the first route down.' He pointed at a spot halfway down the gulch. 'There's a point here where we can see your route and if there's trouble ahead, we'll signal to you. If everything looks fine, we'll join you.'

He drew a line between the two gulches, although in reality there wasn't an easy way to complete this journey.

'Where do we wait for you?'

'You don't.' Sebastian considered. 'Keep going no matter what happens. If you hear gunfire, get down as fast as you can and then keep going.'

For long moments the two men looked at each other until Virgil gave a determined nod. He even glanced at Chuck with approval.

Then, with Temperance having quietened, Sebastian mounted up and joined Chuck. He and Virgil had spoken in low tones and Chuck gave no sign that he'd overheard their conversation. In fact he looked aggrieved while Temperance's smile suggested he'd come off second-best in the argument.

When all the wagons had reached the

summit, at a slow pace they trundled along the ridge. Between the two stretches of lower ground that created the hump, the top of the ridge was flat and around a hundred yards wide, but with precipitous drops on either side everyone had to be careful.

Sebastian rode on ahead and, with him moving away from Virgil and Temperance, Chuck joined him. As they moved on, Sebastian looked back frequently to ensure everyone was safe, but he let a gap build and before long Chuck took the lead and the gap grew even wider.

After thirty minutes Hangman's Gulch came into view and so Sebastian waved at Virgil to let him know they'd reached the area he'd mapped out. Then he hurried on to draw in directly behind Chuck.

He reached him as Chuck passed a sentinel rock that marked the entrance to the gulch. Then he followed Chuck as he picked his way down the gently sloping top of the gulch.

The route would become trickier further down, but the easy start let Chuck and Sebastian move on quickly. By the time that Virgil was close to the sentinel rock, they'd built up a two-hundred-yard gap.

Chuck hadn't looked back for a while and so Sebastian willed him to keep going so that they could move out of sight of the wagons, but on a high point Chuck stopped and faced the top of the ridge. Within a few minutes Virgil would move past the sentinel rock, revealing Sebastian's duplicity and so Sebastian moved on to stand beside Chuck where he considered how he could distract him.

He peered down the gulch as if looking for the best route down, but Chuck ignored him and continued to face the wagons. Sebastian dismounted.

'Is that where Eleazer's hiding?' he asked, pointing.

Chuck glanced down the gulch before returning to looking up at Virgil's wagon, which was slowing down before the large rock, presumably so Virgil could give the others instructions.

'Nope,' Chuck said in a distracted manner.

'Then where is he?' He waited, but Chuck didn't turn. 'If you know, you need to tell me.'

'I know, but I'm not giving you a chance to stop him.'

'You won't know this, but I saw the aftermath of the last raid in the gulch. I know that I can do nothing.'

Chuck grunted and then, with the wagons bunching up, he dismounted and joined him. The two men moved on to a flat boulder where they stood close to a drop of around fifty feet that gave them a good view of the route they'd have to take.

Chuck roved his finger from side to side, marking out the journey until he'd reached a point that was out of their view where presumably the raid would take place. Then he chuckled.

'You're right,' he said with a grin.

'The settlers won't stand a chance.'

Sebastian reckoned that if Chuck turned now he'd see that the train wasn't following them down and so he forced down his disgust and provided an unconcerned smile.

'Why go to all this trouble for a bunch of no-worth settlers?'

'That's not your concern.'

Chuck started to turn and so Sebastian raised his voice.

'You mean you don't know.'

Chuck turned back and slapped a firm finger against his chest.

'You don't understand and I don't reckon you'll live for long enough to work it out. It's better not to know and asking questions don't get you nothing.'

'But you must be curious.' He watched Chuck furrow his brow, but at least he'd got his attention and so he continued. 'You batter people who owe Denver Fetterman money, but one day someone will retaliate and it won't be Denver on the receiving end.'

'Denver pays me well,' Chuck muttered.

'But there's always other opportunities, especially for men who don't want to spend their lives doing another man's bidding.'

That proved to be the wrong angle to take as Chuck waved a dismissive hand at him.

'I prefer living to dying.' Chuck considered the gorge below before swinging round to look up.

Sebastian grabbed his arm and swung him back before he could notice that half of the wagons had moved on past the sentinel rock.

'You don't know what living is,' he said, speaking quickly to keep Chuck's interest, 'if you're always one step away from dying.'

Chuck laughed. 'You'd know all about that.'

'What does that mean?'

Chuck's eyes glazed, as if he'd said too much. Then he tore his arm away and turned, this time in a purposeful manner that Sebastian couldn't stop. He considered the scene above where all but the trailing two wagons had moved on by and Virgil's lead wagon was trundling out of view.

With an angry grunt, Chuck rounded on Sebastian.

'Why are they heading past Hangman's Gulch?' he muttered.

Sebastian smiled. 'Because it's dangerous down here.'

Chuck slowly shook his head. 'I didn't reckon you'd have the guts to defy Denver, but at least you won't have to regret your treachery for long.'

Before Sebastian could retort, Chuck leapt at him. He hit him in the chest with a leading shoulder and knocked him backwards, sending him reeling across the boulder to the edge and the fifty-foot drop beyond.

7

Sebastian dug in a heel and then glanced down, seeing that he'd stopped with his foot on the edge of the boulder. Then he kicked off, but he covered only a short distance before running into Chuck's chest.

Chuck bundled him away with ease, making Sebastian skid backwards, knowing that at any moment he could tip over the edge. So, in desperation, he scrambled to the side, but his foot landed on air. Then he dropped.

With a jarring thud he landed on his right knee with his left leg dangling over the edge and he had to still his momentum by grabbing a protruding rock. Then he looked up as the sole of Chuck's raised boot came hurtling towards his face.

He flinched away, but the kick still connected with his shoulder and sent him tumbling. The next he knew he was slipping over the edge of the boulder and then he was falling.

Sebastian suffered a dizzying view of the ground seemingly rushing up to meet him. Then his flailing hands brushed against the rockface and his fingers found purchase.

With a jolting lurch that swung him in to the rockface he came to a halt. When he took stock of his situation, he found that he'd grabbed the trailing root of a stunted tree that had gathered a precarious hold beneath the lip of the boulder.

He hadn't fallen far, but he couldn't find his footing and his legs only wheeled ineffectually; the root was all that was keeping him from falling. Then above him, Chuck shouted.

'Come back,' he called, his voice echoing in the gulch below. 'The best route is down here!'

Chuck repeated his order three more times. Then he grunted with irritation and a shadow flittered on the lip of the boulder as Chuck came to the edge.

Chuck leaned forward, clearly expecting to see that Sebastian had tumbled to his death, before his gaze centred on him dangling below. He smiled. Then he drew his gun.

Sebastian carried out the only action open to him and he ducked down. The motion pressed him to the rockface and moved him under the lip of the boulder.

The lip was only two feet wide, affording him little protection, but Chuck didn't risk leaning too far over. A scrambling noise sounded as he knelt down. Then a shadow moved across the rockface a moment before gunfire exploded.

The shot was poorly aimed, suggesting that Chuck was firing blind and so Sebastian made it harder for him by shifting his weight. As Chuck fired a second time, he swung himself away from the gun and to his relief this shot missed him too. Even better, his foot found a projection to rest on.

With his body angled away from Chuck, he heard and saw two more gunshots kick splinters away from the rockface before Chuck relented. He heard him pace around above, presumably as he looked for him falling to the ground.

In a moment Chuck would shoot again and so Sebastian sought out another foothold. He found a projection two feet above the first one. He raised his dangling leg to this ledge and then he was able to push his body upwards until his head and shoulders were pressed tightly beneath the lip of the boulder.

With his head cocked on one side he could look forward and so he saw Chuck's arm slip down again. Chuck still wasn't sure where he was hiding and this time he aimed at a point further down the rockface.

Sebastian didn't intend to let him keep trying until he got lucky and, with his body wedged beneath the boulder, he slipped his free hand down to his holster. As Chuck fired, he dragged his gun between his body and the rockface and brought it up to his other hand.

Chuck raised his gun and fired at a point where his quarry's legs had been dangling a few moments earlier, but by then Sebastian had cocked the gun. From only a foot away he aimed at Chuck's wrist.

He waited until Chuck raised his gun again and the barrel was closing in on his body. Then he fired.

A bellow of pain sounded and the gun dropped from view as Chuck jerked his hand away. Then as footfalls stomped away, Sebastian slotted the cocked gun back into his belt and put his free hand to the lip of the boulder.

When he'd gathered a firm grip, he brought his other hand up to the lip. That motion swung his right leg away from the rockface, but he kept his left foot on the foothold.

Then he pushed down, but he managed only to reduce the strain on his arms and he couldn't raise himself.

Something splashed on the back of his hand, the dampness warning him of what would happen next.

Chuck appeared, staring down at him with his blooded hand held against his chest. He met Sebastian's gaze. Then he raised a boot, the action at least giving Sebastian a warning and so, with his weight supported on his foot, he shifted his right hand to the side.

The boot crunched down a finger's width from his hand. Chuck tried again and then again, but each time Sebastian jerked his hand aside and the boot landed on rock.

For his next attempt Chuck took his time. He raised his foot for only a few inches as he tried to predict how far Sebastian would move his hand, but the extra time let Sebastian plan his response.

The moment he saw in Chuck's eyes that he was ready to stamp, he snatched his right hand away, but this time he lowered it to his belt and then swung his gun up. Chuck saw what he planned

98

to do and in retaliation he shifted his weight to his other foot and then raised his boot over Sebastian's left hand, the only one holding him up.

He stamped down. With both men committed to their next act, Sebastian jerked his arm straight up quickly and fired as Chuck's heavy boot came down squarely on his fingers.

Pain shot up through his arm and his eyes became unfocused as he struggled to keep his grip. Only Chuck's weight trapping his fingers against the rock kept him from falling. Then the pressure lifted from his hand and Chuck swayed, his chest blooded, before he tumbled forward and over the edge.

As thuds sounded below, Sebastian shoved his gun hand up to the ledge and slapped the weapon down on the rock. Then he supported his weight while he flexed his bruised fingers and worked out how he could get back up before his strength gave out.

He tried pushing himself higher, but

he was already at full stretch and so he raised his dangling leg and, after scraping his boot along the rockface, he found another foothold. With two feet now braced, he pushed and the pressure on his arms relented for long enough to let him plant his elbows on the boulder.

Then, it was but a few moments before he rolled onto the level ground. He gathered his breath before checking on Chuck's fate, seeing him lying still on his back having fallen and then rolled for several hundred feet. The cloud of dust from his passage still swirled.

At the top of the ridge, the train had moved out of sight, but Sebastian still scurried back up the slope. When he'd checked that nobody was coming back to investigate the gunfire, he returned and mounted up.

Eleazer might have heard Chuck shouting, but unless he checked, Sebastian couldn't know for sure. So he turned towards the lower section of

Hangman's Gulch and, at a steady pace, he headed off.

Chuck's directions had given Sebastian the impression that Eleazer would launch the ambush along a stretch of the gulch where the sheer-sided walls on either side gave the raiders cover and a massive advantage. The only defence was one that was open only to someone who knew the area and who wasn't leading wagons through the narrow pass.

So, after traversing half the route down the gulch, Sebastian took a high path where he dismounted and moved from rock to rock. When the base sloped away from him, he gradually gained height.

The journey to the entrance was two miles long and, with the path becoming more treacherous, it took him fifteen minutes to cover the next hundred yards. He stopped to reconsider.

He decided he'd have to take more chances. He worked his way up to a high point where he could see along both edges of the gulch, but still he couldn't see where Eleazer and his men had holed up.

His higher position let him hear something, although the sounds were distant and hard to discern. He strained his hearing and the light wind brought to him the sound of men shouting. Then came the distinctive rattle of gunfire.

He peered into the gulch, but saw no movement. Then, with a lurch of the stomach, he accepted that the gunfire was raging far beyond Hangman's Gulch along the route that the settlers had taken.

Clearly when Chuck had shouted, Eleazer had heard him and now the raiders had moved on. Heedless now of the danger of being seen, he picked his way back to his horse.

Protected on either side by rock, as he rode down into the gulch he could no longer hear anything. He couldn't stop himself peering up the sides, but nobody waylaid him, forcing him to accept that Eleazer had gone.

He reached the entrance to the gulch without mishap, but a frustratingly lengthy period had passed since he'd heard gunfire and so it was with trepidation that he turned towards the route the wagons had taken.

He speeded to a gallop. He had used the alternate route only once before and so couldn't remember which landmarks to look for, but as it turned out the path the wagons had taken was obvious.

Wheel tracks marked the soft ground at the base of the ridge along with accompanying hoof prints that suggested his worst fears had materialized. He fought down his anger and turned away from the ridge.

He listened intently. He heard no sounds other than the wind, so he set off towards Independence, moving so quickly he didn't even dally to check he was still following the tracks.

All the time he peered ahead, expecting to come across the wagons quickly, but twenty minutes passed and he'd settled into a slower, more sustainable pace before something caught the light. The object was a quarter-mile ahead and to his side and so he slowed to a canter.

The object appeared to be a short pole set into the ground with something leaning against it. He was a hundred yards away when, with a jarring change of perspective, he saw that he'd been wrong. He was in fact approaching a depression and the pole was a large one standing in the centre on a high point.

A man had been strapped to the pole, the form glistening and leaning forward.

Sebastian stopped and stared at the man in horror before his gaze took in the rest of the depression where the tops of tipped-over wagons were visible. He looked further afield, but the surrounding area was devoid of movement and so he dismounted and with his head lowered, he moved on.

The rest of the depression opened up to reveal the ten wagons lying on their sides in a rough circle. There was plenty of movement, but nobody was looking out for anyone approaching.

The settlers had chosen a poor place to make a stand, but when he was fifty yards from the lip of the depression, Sebastian was close enough to understand the situation and he accepted they'd had no choice.

The raiders had overwhelmed the settlers and now they were holding them prisoner.

8

The man tied to the pole was Virgil Michigan. He'd been beaten.

His treatment had encouraged the settlers to fight back, but their defence had failed. Two settlers had been knocked to the ground and now the raiders were ordering the rest to get down on their knees.

With his head down, Sebastian shuffled closer until he reached the lip of the depression where he lay on his chest. He picked a spot that let him see between two wagons and to his shock this revealed a body lying sprawled beside them. On the other side of the camp another body lay face down; both men were from the settlers' camp.

He didn't see any injured raiders. Amelia had said she and the marshal had been attacked by about ten men; Sebastian counted ten newcomers.

They were led by the tall Eleazer Fremont, who was standing back from proceedings, considering the scene from under a lowered hat.

Something about his tense posture made Sebastian reckon he'd seen him before, but he couldn't recall when. Belongings had been strewn across the ground and two men were systematically searching through them.

After they'd been through the current set of meagre possessions and then looked inside the wagon itself, they turned to Eleazer and shook their heads.

'Nothing,' one man said.

Eleazer waved them on. Then, with a quick hand gesture, he ordered the settlers to be grouped together.

Five men stood guard around them while the remaining two stood before Virgil. They flexed their fists and rolled their shoulders, as if preparing to resume beating their prisoner again, but Eleazer bade them to back away so he could stand before Virgil alone.

'Talk,' he said, his voice low but carrying around the site.

'I don't know what you want,' Virgil said with his head lowered.

Eleazer glanced at his fist and rolled his shoulders, making Virgil turn his head away, but then he lowered the hand and backed away, settling for having delivered his threat.

'Then,' he said with a smirk, 'we'll keep searching.'

Eleazer gestured at the men looking through the belongings, ordering them to be more thorough. So they made a show of hurling items around, although, from their irritated grunts, they made no progress.

This development intrigued Sebastian as it appeared to confirm that Denver Fetterman hadn't sent Eleazer after the settlers to steal their valuables. Instead, he was interested in something specific, even if it was unclear what it was.

The settlers' frightened postures suggested that they might not know what was wanted; it might even be owned by Jeremiah.

Sebastian shook these thoughts away when the searching men moved on to the next wagon, which was the one directly in front of him. This took them out of his view and, other than clothes flying into the air, he couldn't see how their search progressed.

He noted that none of the other raiders was looking his way. So he rolled over the lip and into the depression. Then he hurried to the back of the nearest wagon where he slipped through a rent in the canvas cover to get inside.

He pressed himself flat to what had been the base. Then, with his gun drawn, he faced the front, waiting for the men to finish their search.

He didn't have to wait long. He had only time to settle his stance when a man peered inside, sporting a bored expression that turned to horror when he found himself looking down the barrel of Sebastian's gun.

Then Sebastian fired, dropping him with a shot to the centre of the chest.

A second man slipped into view as he tried to stop the first man from falling over, and Sebastian made him pay for his mistake with a deadly shot to the neck. Then he hurried out of the wagon and made his way to the next, where he moved along to the front and peered around the corner.

As he'd hoped, his intervention had given the settlers hope. Clement Wainwright had taken on his guard while the others were adding to the confusion by fleeing.

Sebastian edged forward to bring the whole depression into view. Eleazer was directing his men to join him in grouping up on the opposite side of the depression where they moved to slip behind two wagons.

Sebastian hurried them on their way with a couple of gunshots that went wild before he hunkered down to reload. When he looked up, a line of settlers was hurrying towards him and he beckoned them on.

They all hurried past except for Temperance, who knelt beside him.

'They caught up with us quickly,' she said. 'We didn't have the time to organize a proper defence before they overwhelmed us.'

'The raiders sure seem determined, but surrender isn't an option. They're looking for something and they won't give up until they find it.'

'I agree.' Temperance shook her head sadly. 'But I have no idea what they're looking for.'

Sebastian believed her, but he reckoned someone would know the answer. Before he could ask someone else, one of the raiders jumped up and blasted lead at him. The shot slew a foot wide, kicking splinters from the base of the wagon and forcing him to back away.

The gunshot encouraged the settlers to spread out around the backs of the wagons. None of them was armed, but thankfully in the centre of the depression Clement had disarmed the raider he'd taken on and he now ran into hiding to Sebastian's right.

Sebastian waved at him to join him in fighting back and so, in a coordinated movement, both men edged out from cover and peppered lead at the raiders. The moment they stopped firing, retaliatory gunfire blasted out.

For the next five minutes both groups traded gunfire without success. This stand-off couldn't continue indefinitely and so with the raiders outnumbering the armed settlers, the next time the raiders peppered gunfire at them Sebastian backed away to consider his alternatives.

The settlers were spread out on either side of him, mostly women and children and, although they all sported grim and determined looks, he couldn't see what they could do other than to stay hidden. So he provided an encouraging smile that didn't represent his feelings at all and moved on to the next wagon.

With his gun holstered, he hurried away from Clement, hoping to gain a different angle and perhaps trap the raiders in a pincer movement. He ran past two wagons without encountering a problem, but there was a lengthy distance to the next one, and so he halted and peered around the corner.

He found himself looking at Virgil; the man was glaring directly at him from the stake. That surprised Sebastian as he'd thought he'd moved stealthily and so he backed away quickly, but then the thought came that maybe Virgil hadn't been looking out for him.

He ducked and turned, the action saving him from a lunging blow aimed at his head from one of the raiders who had used his ruse of sneaking into a wagon. His assailant had tried to swipe him with his gun hand and so Sebastian grabbed his wrist.

The two men scuffled until Sebastian jerked the man's wrist to the side. The motion was quick enough to tear the gun from his grip and send it clattering to the ground.

The man quickly got his wits about him and lunged for Sebastian's holster, forcing Sebastian to twist his hip away. But his foot caught on the protruding brake lever and he stumbled backwards.

As they were entangled, he dragged the man down with him and they both went tumbling out into clear space.

On the ground the man fought to keep Sebastian's hands away from his gun while keeping him pinned down. Sebastian didn't mind this tactic as they were in full view of the raiders across the depression and the moment he fought his way clear he could be shot.

They struggled, with neither man getting the upper hand. Then, when people started shouting nearby, his assailant moved up Sebastian's body and settled a knee on his hip. Then he released one of Sebastian's hands, thumped him in the stomach, and then threw himself aside.

Sebastian had expected him to try to grab his gun and so he scrambled round to lie on his side with his holster beneath him, but then he saw that the man had gained his feet. Unsure of his opponent's next move Sebastian rolled twice in the opposite direction and then used his momentum to get to his feet.

Then, with his head down, he ran into cover behind the nearest wagon where he swirled round, expecting to face his opponent, but instead, he saw the man running past Virgil in the middle of the depression.

Sebastian levelled his gun on his back, but he didn't fire when he saw that the other raiders were slipping over the lip of the depression. A few moments later several settlers uttered ragged cheers, confirming that the raiders were retreating.

Sebastian still waited with his gun trained on the lip beyond the wagons while the settlers stayed behind their cover. Several minutes later he saw movement, but it was some distance away and so he scrambled up the side of the depression where he saw only a retreating dust cloud heading south.

He returned to the settlers, but the good news didn't cheer the survivors. Two were dead and Virgil had been beaten badly. Sebastian joined the group that rushed to cut Virgil down.

'Do you know what they wanted?' Sebastian asked.

'No,' Virgil murmured through blooded lips, 'but I'm sure they didn't find it.'

Sebastian winced. 'That means they'll be back.'

Virgil nodded and then stood still as a knife was produced to slice through the ropes that bound his hands behind his back. Sebastian stood back to let them free Virgil and his new position let him see movement from the corner of his eye.

He swirled round to see that Eleazer Fremont had sneaked back. He was standing crouched on the edge of the depression with his gun raised.

Sebastian threw a hand to his holster, but he was too late. Eleazer fired, the shot making everyone turn on the spot as they sought out the shooter, but before anyone got their wits about them, Eleazer ducked down from view.

A few moments later his form appeared, but this time he was on horseback and beating a hasty retreat. His last act had seemed a pointless act of defiance, but then Temperance came running across the depression, her face contorted with panic.

Sebastian swirled round and he felt his cheeks twitch as his mouth fell open in horror. Virgil was standing with his head rocked back, a reddening hole in the centre of his forehead.

Then he slumped forward to slump lifelessly against the stake.

★   ★   ★

Sebastian drew his horse to a halt on a rise and looked down into the valley beyond.

Seven years had passed since he'd left Independence, and he'd never thought he'd see the settlement again. To his surprise the sight of the few dozen buildings nestling in the valley below made him relax for the first time since the raid.

Despite everyone's concern about what Eleazer Fremont would do next, he hadn't returned. The settlers had travelled quickly, completing a three-day journey in two days. All the time they'd posted outlying riders to look out for approaching trouble, but nobody had seen any sign of a pursuit.

The deaths of three settlers meant that the group had stayed subdued and, as the wagons drew up into a line on either side of him, the sight of their destination gained nothing more than sighs of relief. With his task now complete, Sebastian rode on to stand alongside Temperance's wagon.

'Despite everything,' he said, 'I hope you can find happiness here.'

'Unlikely,' Temperance murmured, her voice catching before she raised her chin with defiance. 'But I hope you can.'

'I'm not coming with you.' He

pointed over his shoulder. 'I'm going back to find Jeremiah and Gabriel.'

'Jeremiah can take care of himself.'

'I'm sure he can, but Eleazer Fremont was looking for something. As he didn't come after us again, he may go after them.'

'None of us own anything. Eleazer won't be interested in . . . '

She trailed off and closed her eyes for a moment, as presumably the same thought hit her that had occurred to Sebastian. Even if she could vouch for the rest of the settlers, she couldn't say the same for Jeremiah, a man who had joined the train later than the others had.

'I'll not rest,' Sebastian said, 'until I've confirmed everyone is safe.'

He provided an encouraging smile, but Temperance hadn't finished with him. She raised her head to consider Independence and then gave him a long stare.

'I heard that the last time raiders attacked settlers on the way to Independence, none of them lived for long enough to enjoy their success.'

'They didn't,' Sebastian said, clenching a fist. 'Our raiders won't either.'

They considered each other in silence, allowing Sebastian to ponder the enormity of the promise he'd just made.

'I hope when this is over,' Temperance said after a while, 'you'll come back. Settling down here will be better for you than pursuing the lost dream of the money that's waiting in Eureka.'

Sebastian looked away, unwilling to admit that the matter still concerned him.

'I told your brother about that in confidence.'

'And I've told nobody else, but he was right, wasn't he? For six months you've never strayed far from Eureka, and that was to keep open the option of returning there one day.'

'You can never go back.' His low tone hadn't sounded convincing, and so he mustered a smile. 'Eureka is as much my land of lost dreams as Independence is.'

'You could be right.' She considered the town ahead and then nodded, as though she'd made a decision. 'And perhaps that applies to me too. I'm going with you.'

9

When Sebastian and Temperance reached the depression where the raiders had attacked the settlers, Sebastian used the knowledge of the area he'd gathered as a young man. He sought out a route to the Devil's Hump that only people travelling light could take.

They made good time over the ridge and they reached the scene of Gabriel's departure from the group by sundown, two days after turning their back on Independence.

During their journey they'd seen nobody and neither had they picked up any tracks other than the signs left by the wagons and the raiders during their ambush.

The next day they continued to backtrack along the route the settlers had taken. Sebastian didn't notice any signs of Jeremiah's search for Gabriel.

Then again, he didn't look too carefully.

He had decided that Temperance had been right. Jeremiah could take care of himself and they could leave him to search for Gabriel.

Sebastian didn't think it worthwhile trying to talk her out of staying with him until he'd completed his mission as she had been as quiet on the journey away from Independence as she had been on the way to it. But he did reckon he had to explain his alternative plan, so when they next stopped for a break, he pointed ahead.

'I'm going after Denver Fetterman in Pearl Forks,' he said.

'Why?' she asked.

'Because Chuck Kelley worked for him.' Sebastian sighed and then explained something he'd avoided talking about so far, albeit using a choice of words that included enough truth to be believable. 'Back in Hangman's Gulch, I worked out Chuck was following Denver's orders by leading us into an ambush. Chuck turned on me. We fought and I killed him.'

'Then,' she said, 'we look for answers with Denver.'

Although Sebastian couldn't let her meet Denver in case she learnt the truth about his role in the ambush, he nodded and tried to avoid worrying about his problem until later.

For the next two days, he remained focused and they reached Pearl Forks without mishap and still without meeting anyone. He figured that Sheriff McSween wouldn't expect him to return and so he rode into town openly and then moved into a position opposite the Long Trail.

'After I've found out the truth from Denver,' he said, 'we'll need to get out of town quickly. So you look after the horses and be ready to move quickly.'

She shot him an aggrieved glare. 'I didn't come all this way to stand outside a saloon.'

'And I didn't come all this way to find out you weren't prepared to work as a team.' He flashed a smile. 'I need your help.'

This declaration appeared to appease her and so they settled into watching the saloon. It was late afternoon and, other than the comings and goings he'd expect, he saw nothing untoward.

So, after confirming where she'd wait, he headed round to the back of the building. The door through which he'd been dragged last week was open, letting him slip inside quickly.

He faced a flight of stairs. He hurried up them and then on to the room in which Denver Fetterman had delivered his ultimatum. There he listened, but heard nobody within and so he entered.

As he expected, Denver's office was deserted. So he waited, sitting on a chair behind the door.

After sundown, sounds of revelry in the saloon drifted up to him and several times people came upstairs, making him tense, but they all went past the office. He'd sat for at least three hours, the wait having made his already tense mood darken, when someone came upstairs and opened the door.

This man stood in the doorway before closing the door behind him; Denver Fetterman had returned to his office. He had his head bowed reading a ledger, which he closed with a firm slap.

The noise masked the sound of Sebastian moving in. He thrust his Peacemaker up against Denver's neck, making him flinch.

'I'm back,' he whispered in Denver's ear.

'Sebastian Ford,' Denver said, speaking at a normal volume, presumably in the hope that he'd be overheard. 'I didn't expect you'd come back, ever.'

'I appreciate your honesty. Keep it up by giving me the answers I want.'

'And as a reward you'll let me go, I presume?'

'No.' Sebastian jabbed the gun into Denver's neck. 'As a reward I won't make you suffer.'

Sebastian pushed Denver across the office until they reached his desk. He bent him double so that his cheek was mashed against the wood and he could look up at him.

'You've seen how many men I can call upon,' Denver said, his voice catching with the first hint of fear. 'Kill me and they'll sure make *you* suffer.'

Sebastian narrowed his eyes. The anger that he'd fought down while he'd been waiting hit him, making the blood hammer in his temples.

'I don't care none about that. Eleazer Fremont killed three settlers and he'd have killed more if I hadn't helped them. Now I'm going to do the same to you, but not before you tell me why those good men died.'

Denver glanced at the gun and Sebastian's trembling trigger finger.

'Eleazer isn't my man,' he said with surprising calmness. 'He did only what he was ordered to do, as did I.'

The last comment had the ring of truth to it and so Sebastian drew his gun hand back an inch.

'And what was he ordered to do?'

127

'I've already told you everything I can.'

Sebastian snorted. 'I understand. You're just like Chuck. You're scared.'

Denver conceded his point with a shrug and then closed his eyes, seemingly resigning himself to a fate that Sebastian no longer knew if he was prepared to deliver. But then movement sounded in the corridor, suggesting that Denver's ploy had been to buy himself enough time for someone to come and investigate.

'We've got trouble, Denver,' someone said in the corridor.

Denver looked up at Sebastian and winked.

'That's Wilson Moore,' he whispered, 'the man who keeps the peace in my saloon. That means you're about to face a whole heap of trouble.'

'I won't,' Sebastian whispered. 'Make him go away.'

'That'll just make him more suspicious.'

With a snarl, Sebastian drew his gun

back and yanked Denver up to a standing position. Then he sat casually on the edge of Denver's desk with the gun held against Denver's back and out of view from the door.

'No tricks,' he said, 'or you'll die first.'

Denver gave a brief nod. Then, with a roll of his shoulders, he gathered his composure.

'Come in and explain,' he said using an irritated tone that promised he'd do Sebastian's bidding, but when the door swung open, Sebastian couldn't help but blink hard with shock.

Wilson was escorting Jeremiah Riddle. The captured man had a furrowed brow and a cut on his forehead.

'This man was acting suspiciously downstairs,' Wilson said. 'You want to question him?'

Sebastian shifted his weight on the desk, making it creak and reminding Denver of his predicament.

'I will,' Denver said. He glanced at Sebastian over his shoulder. 'But I'm busy, so make this quick.'

Wilson shoved Jeremiah inside and then stood in the doorway with his gun trained on his back.

'You heard Denver,' he said. 'Explain yourself.'

'I was looking for someone,' Jeremiah said, speaking slowly, his failure to look at Sebastian doing the job of naming that person.

Denver nodded and then spread his hands.

'Is that person up here?'

Jeremiah must have noted the tension in the room as he hesitated before replying and then he gestured angrily at Sebastian.

'He sure is,' he muttered.

'So you followed me,' Sebastian said before Denver could reply.

'I reckoned Gabriel and Amelia found the marshal's horse.' Jeremiah snorted his breath through his nostrils. 'But then I saw you at a distance heading to Pearl Forks, so I followed you to town and then here. I hoped you might have had better luck finding Gabriel.'

Jeremiah's surprisingly subtle answer that avoided mentioning Temperance made Sebastian smile.

'I saw nothing of him, but I doubt he'd have come here.'

'So what are you plotting up here with that man?'

Jeremiah took a long pace forward, forcing Wilson to follow him and place a hand on his shoulder. He moved to drag him backwards, but that brought him close enough for Jeremiah to lash out. His swirling backhanded blow caught Wilson with a stinging slap to the cheek, rocking his head to the side.

Jeremiah shook himself, seemingly only then noticing the danger he was in. He turned on his heel and followed through by grabbing Wilson's gun hand and dragging it to the side.

As the two men tussled and the gun swung up and down, Sebastian moved aside so that he was no longer hiding the gun he held on Denver. Then he slipped off the desk and held Denver securely while he waited to see who got the upper hand.

Jeremiah walked Wilson backwards until he thudded against the wall. Then a gunshot blasted, making Sebastian train his gun on the two men. But it was Jeremiah who stepped backwards. Wilson slid down the wall to sit slumped before he keeled over onto his side.

Jeremiah tapped Wilson's chest with the toe of his boot. When he didn't move, he turned with Wilson's gun in hand and then paced across the office to square up to Sebastian.

'You abandoned the settlers and returned to Pearl Forks real fast to meet with this nobody,' he said, gesturing at Denver. 'I've never trusted you and I reckon you know something about what happened to my son. You'll tell me what it is.'

With Jeremiah having misread the situation so badly, Sebastian struggled to find an appropriate response, but Jeremiah's question made Denver shuffle from foot to foot uncomfortably.

'So this man was with the settlers?' he asked, looking at Sebastian.

'He was,' Sebastian said, 'so you can see why he's angry.'

Denver winced, making Jeremiah advance on him.

'I knew I'd get an answer from one of you,' he muttered, levelling his gun on Denver's chest. 'Speak now or never speak again.'

Denver considered him nervously, clearly noting that Jeremiah looked more determined than Sebastian had been. He even shot a glance at Sebastian, perhaps in the hope that he'd intervene.

Sebastian shook his head, but just then rapid footfalls sounded on the stairs and then in the corridor.

As Jeremiah glanced over his shoulder, Denver took that as his opportunity to act. He threw himself down onto his desk, flattening his body to the wood while his outstretched hand reached for the top drawer.

He had yet to open the drawer when Jeremiah turned and fired. His slug hammered into Denver's side, making him arch his back before he slumped down to lie sprawled over the desk. Then slowly he slid off the desk to lie in a heap on the floor.

Jeremiah considered him with disgust and then hurried to the doorway where he peered out briefly into the corridor. When he looked back across the office, his worried expression confirmed they faced a fight to leave the saloon. Sebastian knelt beside Denver and turned him over onto his back where he lay staring up at the ceiling with glazed eyes.

'You didn't deserve a quick end,' Sebastian said.

Denver's eyes didn't move and Sebastian thought he had already died. But then his chest tensed and he spoke, his voice no louder than a wheezing breath.

'Neither do you.' He gulped. Then his head lolled to the side and his half-closed eyes considered him. 'You'll be running for the rest of your short life.'

'Who?' Sebastian waited, but Denver merely forced a thin smile. 'Tell me, damn you; who are you scared of? Who ordered Eleazer to attack the settlers?'

'It was . . . ' Denver chuckled, the sound a death rattle in the back of his throat. 'It was the man who wants you dead: Dawson Breen.'

10

'I have no choice but to trust you,' Jeremiah said when Sebastian joined him beside the door. 'But the moment we're free, I want answers.'

'You've got nothing to fear from me,' Sebastian said.

Jeremiah swirled round and sneered before he pointed out into the corridor.

'You can start earning my trust again,' he muttered, 'by telling me how we get out of here.'

Sebastian listened to the men moving around at the top of the stairs and then pointed to the right.

'The same way I came in,' he said. 'There's two sets of stairs; the other set leads out to the back.'

'You know plenty for a man who was in town for only a few days.'

Sebastian didn't reckon he had enough time to argue his innocence, as

orders were being given at the top of
the stairs. He moved past Jeremiah so
that he could see into the corridor,
confirming that nobody had come close
yet. Then he looked in the other
direction to see that the route to the
other stairs was clear.

'I'll lead,' he whispered. 'Move fast
and keep your head down.'

He fired blind to the left while
turning to the right. Then, with his
head down, he sprinted for the corner.

He didn't dally to check that
Jeremiah followed, but when he'd
passed two of the four doors on the
corridor, rapid footfalls pattered behind
him. The men at the other end of the
corridor didn't shoot at him and so
when he reached the corner he moved
on for two more steps until he was
against the wall and then glanced back.

Jeremiah was ignoring his instructions and shuffling along sideways with
his gun trained down the corridor
keeping the other men from venturing
out. Then he disappeared from view as

Sebastian pounded along the next corridor.

The stairs and the short corridor at the bottom were in darkness with only reflected light from upstairs to light his way. So he slowed and then took the stairs cautiously with one hand on the rail.

Despite his slow speed, with his gaze set on the door below, he missed his footing and went clattering down several steps until he righted himself. He came to a halt looking back up.

Jeremiah was at the corner peering down the corridor with his gun thrust forward. Sebastian moved on, but he'd managed only another two steps when someone moved in the darkness below.

Instinctively he ducked while turning and his action saved him from a gunshot that whistled by his head and then sliced into the ceiling. The movement unbalanced him and he tried to keep his footing, but his boot missed the step and his hand slipped from the rail.

The next he knew he was tumbling head over heels down the stairs. With no way to stop himself he drew his arms in. Then he rolled on until he slammed down onto the floor and barrelled into someone, who then clattered down on top of him.

He'd come to a shuddering halt when he realized that he'd rolled into the gunman, who was now lying at the bottom of the stairs while Jeremiah hurried on to take advantage of the situation. Sebastian shook himself and then got to his feet groggily where he faced two more men stepping out of the shadows.

Only then did he realize that when he'd fallen he'd dropped his gun and so he leapt at the nearest man. His uncertain gait let the man step to the side and avoid his lunge. Then the man helped him on his way by slapping his back and shoving him towards the wall.

Sebastian got his wits about him fast enough to throw up his hands and cushion the impact. Then he took a moment to shake his head and centre his balance before he swung round.

His assailant was already aiming a blow at the back of his head and so Sebastian jerked away from it. This time the man hammered his fist into the wall.

His assailant grunted in pain and Sebastian added to his discomfort by grabbing the back of his head and slamming his forehead against the wall. He repeated the action and then kicked the man's legs from under him before he turned away.

He found that Jeremiah had come down the stairs. He was tussling with the man Sebastian had tripped up while the other standing man was jigging from side to side, looking for an opening.

The man got his chance when Jeremiah slammed a fierce uppercut into his opponent's chin that sent him reeling into the corner post. His head collided with a thud and he went down heavily. Jeremiah then turned quickly, ducked under an aimed blow from the other man, and headed back to the stairs.

The man moved after him and so Sebastian followed hurriedly and gave him the same treatment that Jeremiah had handed out. By the time the man had rebounded from the corner post and had hit the floor, Jeremiah had reached the bottom of the stairs and was holding out Sebastian's gun.

Sebastian took the weapon. Then they hurried out into the night. Behind them, people bustled in the saloon while distant raised voices showed that others would soon get involved.

'What now?' Jeremiah asked.

'We leave town,' Sebastian said. He turned away from the sounds of the commotion when he saw Temperance riding closer from out of the gloom.

Jeremiah considered her with bemusement and then nodded.

'Escape first,' he said, 'you'll explain later.'

★   ★   ★

Midnight found the three people holed up in the best cover they could find of a dried-up wash ten miles out of town.

Since fleeing the saloon, they'd seen no signs of a pursuit. That didn't mean there wouldn't be one and so Sebastian expected that tonight would be fraught. Then tomorrow they'd face a long day of travelling quickly, all the while looking over their shoulders.

With the seriousness of the situation, since fleeing they hadn't discussed the events in the Long Trail, but Sebastian wasn't surprised that Jeremiah was the one who broke the silence.

'It's later now,' he snapped, turning away from his consideration of the terrain back to Pearl Forks to glare at Sebastian. 'Explain.'

'We shouldn't argue amongst ourselves,' Temperance said with a weary tone before Sebastian could reply. 'You should have accepted by now that Sebastian is on our side.'

Jeremiah didn't reply and so Sebastian shuffled closer to them.

142

'Why do you think I'm against you, Jeremiah?' he asked.

'Back at the Devil's Hump I got chased for several days,' Jeremiah said. 'I barely escaped with my life. Then, despite Virgil's orders for everyone to carry on to Independence, I find you and Temperance back here. Those events don't sound right.'

'They don't.' Sebastian paused to look at him in the low moonlight, giving him a hint that he was about to deliver bad news. 'A raider called Eleazer Fremont attacked the wagon train beyond the Devil's Hump. That chase ended more disastrously than yours did.'

Jeremiah gulped. 'How many?'

'Most of the settlers are fine. After the raid, I led them to Independence, but Milton Burke and Ralph Crowther had been shot and killed.' Sebastian took a deep breath. 'Virgil Michigan was the last to die.'

While Temperance lowered her head, Jeremiah winced and then looked back over the edge of the wash to check that all was still.

'What did Eleazer want?' he asked, his tone distracted.

'He took no supplies, no valuables, no nothing. He was looking for something, and I reckon he didn't find it.'

'Why?'

'Because afterwards he went after you.'

Jeremiah hunched his shoulders and, although there was no sign of a pursuit, he didn't look at them.

'Talking won't help us,' he said, his voice gruff. 'My boy's still missing. You two can do what you want now, but he's my responsibility.'

'He is,' Temperance said, speaking slowly with a lowered tone, 'but you know something about this, don't you?'

Jeremiah rounded on them, but when they both met his gaze, he lowered his head. He fidgeted, seemingly considering whether to answer until, with an angry gesture, he yanked a folded sheaf of papers out of an inside pocket. He considered the papers with his upper lip curled in disgust and then tossed them to the ground.

'Eleazer would have been looking for these,' he murmured.

Temperance picked up the papers, but in the poor light the small writing was impossible to read.

'What are they?'

'My gold mine.' Jeremiah shrugged. 'Well, my sixteenth share in a gold mine's profits.'

'You never mentioned this,' Temperance said, holding out the papers.

'That's because it don't matter none.' Jeremiah snatched the papers from her hand and slipped them back in his pocket. 'It's only money and that can't buy you nothing you want.'

'As Milton, Ralph and my brother found out.'

Sebastian braced himself for Jeremiah's ire, but he provided only a sorrowful nod before he slumped down to sit on the ground.

'I lived in a settlement with three other families and we were content,' he said with his head bowed and his voice so low the others had to sit close beside him to hear. 'One day we struck gold. We weren't looking for it and we didn't know what to do, but the men who came later did.'

'They bought you out?' Sebastian prompted when Jeremiah said no more.

Jeremiah nodded. 'They were more reasonable than we expected. They made us an offer where we had to do nothing in return for a quarter of the profits. We accepted the deal, but then our problems started. The Wilde family got killed by men looking for the money they hadn't received yet. They were the lucky ones.'

'What can be worse than that?'

'Living can. The Shepherd family got excited about the riches to come. They changed, for the worse.' Jeremiah waved a hand, seemingly dismissing them from his thoughts. 'The Parker family started going the same way. I couldn't let that happen to my family. I packed up, moved out and later joined up with Virgil's wagon train.'

Jeremiah looked up and considered Temperance, his jaw grinding and his eyes blank.

'What happened wasn't your fault,' Temperance said. 'I assume other people got to know about what you had, even if we didn't.'

'Perhaps someone overheard me arguing with Florence and Gabriel.' Jeremiah sighed. 'I didn't want them to mix with the kind of men who think the dollar is all that matters.'

Jeremiah looked Sebastian up and down with contempt, but Sebastian couldn't help but smile.

'Except you kept the papers, so — '

'I don't have to explain myself to you. I tried to reason with Florence, but she wouldn't listen. So I left her and tried to save the boy.' Jeremiah slapped a fist into his palm. 'And until you arrived I was winning that battle.'

'I only spoke with him a few times.

You can't blame me for that.' Sebastian waited until Jeremiah's eyes opened wide as he registered who he did blame, and then continued. 'All that matters is what we do now, and I know where Gabriel's gone.'

'How can you know where . . . ?' Jeremiah trailed off and then thumped the ground in frustration. 'He'll have gone to Eureka to look for his mother.'

They sat in silence until Temperance asked the obvious question.

'Which leaves us to decide whether we all go looking for him first,' she said, 'or we go looking for the men who killed our friends?'

'We do both,' Sebastian said before Jeremiah could reply. He stood to look away from Pearl Forks towards his own land of lost dreams. 'Because we'll find them all in the same place.'

11

Eureka was as bustling as Sebastian remembered it, giving him hope that he could ride into town without being noticed. Then again, Dawson Breen and his many eyes would never expect he'd be so stupid as to return here.

On the way, although they'd seen no sign of pursuit, Jeremiah had been tense as he struggled to keep his anger in check. With him being quiet, Sebastian and Temperance had got into the habit of chatting and so, when they drew up on the outskirts of town, Temperance turned to Sebastian.

'This time you'll need all the help you can get,' she said, 'so you're not leaving me in charge of the horses.'

'I won't,' Sebastian said with a smile. 'I reckon we need a base where we can take stock of the situation before we look for Gabriel.'

149

'Agreed.' Temperance looked at the Green Star Hotel a hundred yards down the main drag. 'We get — '

'You two can do what you want,' Jeremiah said interrupting. 'I'm finding my son.'

Jeremiah scowled at them before moving his horse on down the road.

'We'll book enough rooms for us all,' Temperance shouted after him, but if Jeremiah heard, he didn't acknowledge her.

Temperance and Sebastian exchanged amused glances at their surly colleague's behaviour before they headed to the hotel. They booked three rooms and then met up in Temperance's room to look out of the window and survey the scene below.

'Where first?' Temperance asked.

'Jeremiah will search Eureka from end to end,' Sebastian said, 'and ask everyone he meets if they've seen Gabriel.'

'While annoying them and getting into several arguments in the process.'

150

Sebastian laughed and then looked to the outskirts of town.

'So we need to do the opposite by being subtle and thinking about what Gabriel would have done when he arrived here.'

Temperance nodded. 'Amelia would have left him the first chance she got, so Gabriel would have been frightened, without a cent to his name, and hungry.'

'But he's also a resourceful young man and the journey here will have made him even more determined to survive and prove he was right to abandon his father.'

'I agree, but I'm not sure that helps us.'

'It does, because I was once in Gabriel's position.' Sebastian pointed to a stable across the road. 'So he'll have taken any work he can.'

As it turned out, Sebastian's guess that Gabriel had come into town using the same route as they had used and had then found work in the first place he'd come across was half-right. The ostler in the stable reported that a young man matching Gabriel's description had indeed asked for work, although he'd provided a different name. He directed them to the store beside their hotel.

'Can it be this easy?' Temperance said as they headed back across the road.

'We're due some luck,' Sebastian said.

Again, he was half-right; Gabriel was working behind the counter in the mercantile. When they walked through the door, he looked at them with horror before scurrying away into a back room.

The owner considered Gabriel's reaction with bemusement and then faced them.

'What do you want?' he asked.

'A word with your young assistant,' Temperance said with a smile.

The owner folded his arms. 'He didn't look as if he wanted a word with you.'

Temperance leaned on the counter. 'For you to defend him so readily, I reckon he's been a good worker, but nobody wants to take him away. His father would like some answers, though.'

The owner considered her placid expression before mustering a nod.

'He's due a break, so you have thirty minutes to talk to him.' The man shrugged. 'Whether he'll talk to you, though, is a different matter.'

Temperance acknowledged this might be the case with a frown. Then she and Sebastian headed into what turned out to be an empty storeroom. Still, they searched it thoroughly before heading outside, where they found Gabriel skulking around behind their hotel.

He was throwing stones at a can he'd set up on a fence post that stood between the mercantile and the hotel. None of the stones troubled the can.

Sebastian stood back to let Temperance take the lead, but she shook her head and beckoned Sebastian to talk to him first. In the end they settled for leaning against the opposite end of the fence.

Their presence worsened Gabriel's aim and, after one stone had winged into the fence beside Sebastian's hand, Gabriel dropped the rest of the stones he'd gathered to the ground.

'Why did you come back for me?' he snapped, swinging round to face them.

'We didn't,' Sebastian said. 'We're killing two birds with one stone.'

He picked up the stone Gabriel had thrown. Then he hurled the stone at the can and knocked it from the post. His success made Gabriel clench his fists until with a snort of laughter he lightened his mood.

'What's your other reason for being here?'

'We have business with Dawson Breen, the owner of the Bonanza House. He hired the raiders who attacked Amelia, and then the wagon train.'

The last comment made Gabriel wince and he moved over to join them in leaning back against the fence.

'Everyone fine?' he asked with genuine concern in his eyes.

'Milton,' Temperance said, 'Ralph and my brother were killed, but the rest are safe, including your father.'

Gabriel breathed a sigh of relief before he shot them a sly glance that appeared to accept he couldn't now claim he didn't care about his father.

'Has he come with you?'

'At the moment he's tearing the town apart,' Sebastian said. 'He won't leave until he knows you're safe.'

'I'm not leaving with him. I'm a man now and I make my own decisions, just like my mother did.'

His voice caught and so Sebastian lowered his tone as he asked the question he didn't need to ask.

'Did you find her?'

'No.' Gabriel kicked at the dirt. 'And Amelia didn't want to stay with me after we arrived here. She wasn't a very nice woman, as you said.'

'Did you find out what she'd done wrong?'

'I tried. She told me several different versions and most of them involved stealing.' He shrugged. 'But at least she was grateful.'

Gabriel couldn't stop a huge grin breaking out, even though he then tried to hide it behind his hand, so Sebastian didn't bother asking how grateful she'd been.

'You do realize this means you can't stay here, don't you?'

'I'm not leaving Eureka.' Gabriel sighed and then stood tall. 'Which means I'll have to help you take on Dawson Breen.'

With Gabriel's final comment effectively admitting he knew why Dawson had organized the raid on the settlers, everyone stood in silence. Sebastian didn't reckon he should be the one who refused Gabriel's help and Temperance's silence suggested she was struggling to find the right reply.

'If we're to take on Dawson,'

Temperance said after a while, 'we'll all have tasks to complete, and we can't make plans while we have the distraction of you and your father being estranged.'

Temperance smiled, letting Gabriel figure out the rest for himself.

'I'll talk with him,' Gabriel said with a long sigh that, to Sebastian's ears, didn't sound as resigned as he tried to make out, 'but I'm helping you no matter what he says.'

Temperance didn't argue with that, although the narrow-eyed glance she shot at Sebastian said that no matter how much Gabriel complained, they'd keep him out of their plans. With that agreement made, she pointed out Sebastian's hotel window and they arranged for Gabriel to join them tonight to meet his father.

'That should be long enough,' Temperance said when Gabriel was heading back into the mercantile, 'for us to talk Jeremiah round to being reasonable.'

Sebastian reckoned Temperance was being optimistic, but he kept that thought to himself and instead, with the solution to one problem in hand, he turned his thoughts to the bigger predicament.

They returned to Temperance's room where he drew her to the window. He explained the lay of Eureka, starting with the area closest to the hotel and ending with the Bonanza House on the far side of town.

'That's Dawson's side of town,' he said, pointing at a large building set apart from the others so that it stood out even from several hundred yards away. 'He owns a smaller saloon on the other side of the road as well as two hotels and several other businesses. We won't be able to get within a hundred yards of him without someone in his employ seeing us.'

'Perhaps you won't, but he's never met me or Jeremiah.'

Sebastian winced, accepting he was the weak link. Despite his comment when they'd ridden into town, he had still wanted to keep her away from trouble. The odds he faced meant that no longer felt possible. But, after all, she had shown tact when she'd persuaded the mercantile owner to let them see Gabriel, so he nodded.

'That means we'll have one shot at this and we'll have to be decisive.'

'And we shouldn't risk looking for Jeremiah until it's dark.'

Sebastian couldn't disagree with this and so he sat at the table beside the window. Using anything he could bring to hand, he created a map of the area. They leaned over the representation and as the afternoon wore on, they knocked ideas back and forth.

Nothing they suggested sounded likely to succeed and, with sundown approaching, Temperance volunteered to leave and find Jeremiah. While she got ready to go, Sebastian looked out of the window and saw that the subject of their discussion was returning.

Jeremiah was walking down their side

of the main drag with his head lowered and his posture indicating defeat. Sebastian wondered if he might accidentally look into the mercantile and resolve the problem of how they introduced him to his son, but he walked by and to the Green Star Hotel, where he went straight inside.

'He's coming up,' Sebastian reported. 'Let's hope we don't spend the rest of the evening arguing.'

Temperance nodded. 'Agreed. The three of us need to work together now.'

She moved over to the door while Sebastian stood by the window.

'And to come up with some good ideas . . . ' Sebastian trailed off and then looked aloft while he thought back. 'We didn't tell Jeremiah which hotel we were going to, but he came straight in here.'

'When we talked about getting a room, this was the nearest hotel.' Temperance shrugged. 'Or perhaps he heard we'd come here.'

'The second possibility is what's worrying me.'

Temperance winced and then threw open the door. She peered out into the corridor before gesturing at Sebastian to join her. They hurried out.

The hotel had only one upper floor, but they were in a corridor with a branch on the other side of the stairs and so they hurried into the other branch. Then they took the only cover they could find by slipping into an alcove.

A few moments later Jeremiah came up the stairs, stomping his feet loudly in his usual fashion, after which he went straight to Temperance's room, knocked, and went in.

Sebastian and Temperance glanced at each other, acknowledging that his behaviour was odd and that they should be cautious. Then, stepping lightly, they hurried along the corridor and down the stairs.

They didn't speak until they'd confirmed that there was nobody on duty downstairs who Jeremiah could have spoken to and to tell him which rooms they'd booked.

'Jeremiah's not a subtle man.' Temperance said. 'While he was finding someone who'd seen us, he'll have barged his way around town and drawn attention to himself.'

'If he mentioned my name,' Sebastian said, 'he might have been followed. We need to leave quickly.'

Temperance nodded and so, side by side, they pushed through the front door. After two paces, they came to a sudden halt. Lined up in the road were five men, four with guns drawn, flanking the man they had come to confront.

'So it appears,' Dawson Breen said with a confident gleam in his eye, 'you've decided to make this easy for me.'

12

Dawson Breen gave Sebastian and Temperance a moment to accept that they'd been defeated. Then he moved backwards for a short pace.

Sebastian had already seen the flicker in Dawson's gaze that meant he was about to direct his men to fire and so before the gunmen could react he turned quickly on his heel.

He shoved Temperance towards the open door, but thankfully she'd reacted quickly too and she gained the doorway at Sebastian's side. Then once inside she hurled herself in the opposite direction to him.

Gunfire still blasted through the open doorway and the shots peppered along the bottom of the stairs until Temperance backhanded the door shut. With only moments to act before the gunmen made their next move, Sebastian looked for a way out, seeing that a corridor led away beside the stairs.

They didn't have enough time to head upstairs to fetch Jeremiah without trapping themselves, but from the corner of his eye he saw that a man was already standing at the top of the stairs. So, as they set off, Temperance gestured at this man to join them in fleeing, presumably because, unlike Sebastian, she hadn't registered that the man wasn't Jeremiah.

Sebastian came to a skidding halt beside the foot of the stairs and stared at Eleazer Fremont, who was standing with his hat drawn low and his posture stooped. Temperance continued running, but Sebastian was rooted to the spot, wondering how long Eleazer had been upstairs and whether he'd listened in on their plans.

Then Eleazer moved his hand towards his jacket, the motion making Sebastian realize he'd met him long before the raid on the settlers.

The shock broke him out of his fugue

and, while ducking to gain the minimal cover of the rails, he followed Temperance, who had now reached a door. As Sebastian made further connections, he moved slowly and so when he reached the door, Temperance looked at him oddly and then slapped him on the back to hurry him on.

They emerged into a lounge with one other door. The light streaming in through a window said that the door led outside. Behind him the gunmen were running into the entrance hall while Eleazer shouted instructions to them about where they'd gone.

'What's wrong?' Temperance asked as they ran across the lounge.

'That was Eleazer Fremont, Dawson Breen's most trusted hired gun.'

As they'd reached the door, Temperance didn't ask how he knew Dawson trusted him the most. Sebastian was pleased as it would take a while to explain how he'd only now pieced together that Eleazer was the gunman who had stood at Dawson's shoulder on the night he'd won sixteen thousand dollars at the poker table.

They stood on either side of the door where Sebastian drew his Peacemaker and Temperance her pistol. She gave him a long look that said she knew how to defend herself. Then they charged out with their heads held low.

Their caution paid off when a burst of gunfire peppered along the hotel wall above their heads. As Sebastian ran towards the fence where earlier they had talked with Gabriel, he picked out the shooters standing further along the fence.

He slowed to move sideways and aimed at the nearest man. On the run he fired and his ill-directed shot tore into a fence post two feet to his target's side, but it was close enough to make the man flinch, letting them hurry on to the fence.

Temperance stopped first and, with her back braced against the wood, she fired. Her accurate gunshot sliced into the second man's stomach and made him fold over the fence. As the man toppled down onto his back on the other side, Temperance swung her pistol to the side to aim at the second man, who had enough time to return fire.

He was no more accurate than Sebastian had been and his shot hammered into the wall. He didn't get to shoot a second time, though, as Temperance got him in her sights and pounded a shot into his chest that stood him upright, his gun falling from his grasp.

A second shot from Sebastian, to the stomach, dropped him. Sebastian tipped his hat to Temperance, making her smile, and then they both slipped through the fence and hurried on.

They'd managed only a few paces when Gabriel emerged from the back door of the mercantile. He cast the fallen men only a cursory glance, showing he must have been watching the altercation from inside. Then, with a smile on his lips, he raised the lids of the two barrels that stood on either side of the door.

'You'll never outrun them,' he said. 'So hide.'

Sebastian's instinct was to run and he hated the thought of being trapped, but Temperance had no such qualms and she clambered inside the nearest barrel without comment. Back in the hotel, Eleazer barked out orders to follow them outside and so with only moments before he was discovered, Sebastian followed Temperance's lead and ducked down into the second barrel.

A moment later Gabriel slammed the lids down. Then, through a crack in the barrel, Sebastian watched him walk towards the fence.

Sebastian shifted his weight so that he could hunker down and he held his gun in a position where he could fire if circumstance forced him to, although he doubted his aim would be accurate.

Gabriel reached the fence and was staring at the bodies with horror when two gunmen burst out of the hotel. They noticed him immediately and Gabriel thrust up his hands while taking a backward pace. Then Eleazer and Dawson came out.

'Who shot them?' Dawson asked Gabriel.

'I . . . I don't know their names,' Gabriel said, his shaking voice sounding convincingly scared, although with the gunmen surrounding him it was likely he wasn't pretending.

'I don't care about their names,' Dawson muttered advancing on Gabriel and making Sebastian in the barrel aim at him. 'I want to know where they went.'

'They ran on past the store.' Gabriel swirled round and pointed while cringing. 'One of them said something about heading to the stables.'

Dawson gave a short nod and so the gunmen slipped through the fence and then ran on past the store and out of Sebastian's view. Dawson and Eleazer stayed where they were.

In the barrel Sebastian firmed his gun arm and willed Dawson to come closer, but instead Dawson backed away. While Eleazer checked out the shot men, he leaned against the fence and glared at Gabriel, who lowered his head.

When Eleazer returned, shaking his head, the two men stood in silence until the hotel door opened and to Sebastian's surprise Amelia Cook came out. Although, once he'd shaken away his shock, her arrival gave him a possible chain of events that had led to Jeremiah being followed.

Gabriel tensed, but Amelia didn't look at him. She joined Dawson and gave him a simpering smile that made Dawson smirk.

'You did well,' he said. 'A woman like you can go far with me.'

Amelia sidled closer and looped an arm into his.

'Anything I can do for you, just ask.'

Dawson chuckled, but when Gabriel's mouth fell open, he extracted himself from her arm and pointed at the store. Gabriel didn't waste a moment before he scurried off. Foot-falls pattered as he ran between the barrels and inside.

Worryingly, Dawson watched him leave with his brow furrowed until with a shake of the head he appeared to dismiss a thought. He turned to Eleazer.

'This situation has dragged on for too long,' he said. 'I want to end this tonight.'

'Do you mean with Sebastian or with the gold?' Eleazer asked.

'Both. Thanks to Amelia I have Jeremiah. All I need now is Sebastian Ford out of the way and I can move on.'

Eleazer rolled his shoulders and then walked off, taking him out of Sebas-tian's view while Dawson stayed with Amelia.

In the barrel, Sebastian edged from side to side, but the thin gap between two planks was the best sighting he could get of Dawson. If he were to fire, with his limbs cramped, he wasn't sure of success. He could even hit Amelia and, despite her duplicity, he couldn't bring himself to risk that.

Even leaping up out of the barrel would waste valuable moments before he could take careful aim, but then his chance disappeared as Dawson took Amelia's elbow and led her away.

Sebastian waited but they didn't come back into view and neither did Eleazer, but the search for them must still be going on, he thought, as he heard the distant sounds of people shouting. So he trusted Gabriel to return and release them when the time was right.

Despite that resolution, Temperance made the first move when, after they'd waited patiently for fifteen minutes, she hissed a question. Sebastian couldn't hear the words, but he didn't need to.

'Wait,' he muttered.

In reply, Temperance squealed. Then

her barrel clattered over and she came scrambling out.

Sebastian figured he shouldn't wait any longer and he clambered out to find Temperance lying on her back massaging her cramped legs. Sebastian hurried over to her and helped her into the store before returning to right the barrels.

Then he peered out through the door, but thankfully nobody was about and so he slipped back inside to find that even though Temperance had now dealt with her cramps, she looked no happier.

'What do we tell Gabriel?' she whispered with a glance across the room to check they were alone.

'Nothing,' Sebastian said. He shuffled closer, checking that the room was empty before he continued. 'We overheard something, but we don't know for sure what it meant.'

'We can work it out, though. Amelia recognized Jeremiah and she told Dawson about him. Dawson waylaid him and then Jeremiah led Dawson to us.'

'I don't like Jeremiah, but I don't believe he'd do that.'

'I do, if Dawson has a hold over him, and I can think of only one thing that'd make a man like him do Dawson's bidding so readily.'

Temperance considered him until Sebastian provided a slow nod.

'His wife Florence ran away in Eureka. Dawson has her.'

'Which is probably how he got to know about the mine.' Temperance shrugged. 'But we can't tell Gabriel that.'

Sebastian couldn't disagree with that and so to give himself time to think through the implications, he looked out through the doorway. A man's shadow was playing across the barrel outside and Sebastian couldn't help but wince when that man moved forward and he saw that it was Gabriel.

'I heard everything,' Gabriel said with a determined tone. 'You can't stop me helping you now.'

Sebastian stopped Temperance when they reached the edge of Dawson's territory. Ahead, the Bonanza House was a massive shining jewel in the night.

Light streamed from every window, making the road and buildings opposite appear as illuminated as if it were high noon, while they'd heard the sounds of revelry and music from the opposite side of town. The establishment had looked like this when Sebastian had last visited it, but this time he noted a small change that made his already tense posture stiffen a little more.

Dawson had renamed the Bonanza House. Now a huge sign across the front of the building proclaimed it to be the Land of Dreams.

'He did that to annoy us,' Temperance muttered.

'No,' Sebastian said. 'He did that to show us he's already won.'

'Then it'll hurt all the more when we defeat him.'

Sebastian patted Temperance's shoulder, enjoying her positive attitude, but standing here for the first time in six months brought home to him how impossible their task was.

Although he'd now accepted she was resourceful and capable in difficult situations, his only other help would come from Gabriel. Worse, Dawson controlled his empire with an iron fist.

Armed guards patrolled outside and checked everyone for weaponry as they entered. Once inside they would be in Dawson's domain where attacking him would be hard and, with the area so well guarded and lit up, getting away afterwards would be even harder.

The toughest element was Dawson's popularity. At some time in the evening most people in town gravitated to his establishment because they liked Dawson and the entertainment he provided.

Nobody appeared to know or care about his nefarious activities and, even if Dawson strayed away from his armed guards, dozens of ordinary people would leap to his defence the moment they tried anything.

'Gabriel should be in position now,' Sebastian said quickly before they drew attention to themselves by staring at the building for too long, 'so let's take Dawson's dream away.'

Temperance nodded and then, without further discussion, they headed off. They joined a lively group that was heading inside where they engaged in animated conversation, as if they were embarking on a friendly night out.

They had to line up to be frisked, which was completed without problems, as they weren't armed. Although they avoided catching anyone's eye, Sebastian reckoned that the guards at the door didn't pay them any more attention than they did to anyone else.

Then they found themselves in the large entrance hall where they had a choice of entertainment they could enjoy.

To the left was a bustling saloon catering for drinkers while to the right was a music hall, although the night's entertainment had yet to get underway and so many people were filling the entrance hall.

Ahead were three gaming rooms. Rowdy and inebriated customers filled the large room to the left, while the smaller room to the right catered for customers who preferred a quieter, more exclusive night with higher stakes. The middle room was guarded and entrance was by invitation only for those who could afford the high-stakes games.

During the evening Dawson visited all parts of his domain, but the middle room was where he usually ended up, although he didn't always gamble. There were stairs on either side of the gaming rooms leading up to bedrooms that were cheap to hire, usually by the hour, and Gabriel should now have taken one.

'Let's do this,' Temperance said, having surveyed the situation and confirmed the scene was as Sebastian had described it.

So, with a nod that said he was ready for trouble, Sebastian joined the short queue of people wanting to cash in their gaming chips. Sebastian's account was so large he'd not needed to keep his winning chips and so once the two people before him had been dealt with, he spread his hands wide apart on the counter and smiled at the cashier.

'My name's Sebastian Ford,' he said. 'And I want my sixteen thousand dollars.'

13

To the cashier's credit, Sebastian's request didn't even make her blink.

'Someone will come,' she said with practised ease, 'and confirm you are who you say you are.'

Then she directed him to stand aside so she could pay the next man his winnings, which turned out to be five dollars and which she paid over with the same level of courtesy as she'd shown Sebastian.

'Are you sure it'll be Dawson?' Temperance whispered when Sebastian had moved away from the counter.

'He wouldn't leave this to anyone else,' Sebastian said, 'and he'll pay, but then we'll have to move quickly.'

Temperance nodded and then sidestepped away to await developments. Her first task, after Sebastian had collected his winnings, was to take possession of the money.

Sebastian hoped that Dawson's attention would be on him and so he wouldn't notice her intervention. Then she would take the money upstairs and pass it on to Gabriel, who would spirit the money away and provide Sebastian with leverage to persuade Dawson to do their bidding.

Beyond that, they had no plans other than to take whatever opportunities came their way and, as it turned out, Dawson didn't keep them waiting for long. He emerged from the middle gaming room with his eyebrows raised in what appeared to be genuine surprise.

Eleazer Fremont didn't accompany him, but flanking him were two guards. These men were a head taller than Dawson and, even if they hadn't been armed, they appeared capable of dealing with Sebastian and Temperance without breaking a sweat.

'I'm pleased you've come to collect your money,' Dawson said, spreading his hands with a magnanimous gesture. 'It's been waiting for you for six months.'

Few of the people milling around in the entrance room paid this meeting any attention, but Dawson's guards settled their stances, presumably preparing to act if Sebastian mentioned Dawson's efforts to ensure he didn't collect.

'Then I won't keep you waiting any more,' Sebastian said with studied good humour, although he raised his voice so that the nearby customers would note his presence. 'I'll take my money and leave peacefully.'

'Of course you can, but I sincerely hope you've organized adequate protection. I wouldn't like my establishment's good reputation to be tarnished if something unfortunate were to happen to you.'

'Thank you for your concern, but rest assured that I intend to leave Eureka safely.'

Dawson tapped his chin, as if

thinking, and then brightened.

'I have an idea. To ensure your safe passage, you could leave with your friends.'

Dawson raised a hand, the gesture seeming to have been pre-arranged as the guards edged apart slightly.

Sebastian wasn't surprised when Eleazer came down the left-hand stairs, but he couldn't help but wince when Jeremiah and a woman, presumably his wife, Florence, followed him down. Worse, behind them trooped Gabriel, his head lowered.

Florence also kept her gaze on the stairs, as if she were worried she might stumble, adding credence to the possibility that she'd been kept prisoner and she wasn't used to crowds. Jeremiah displayed none of his usual surly attitude and he took great care in guiding her along.

At the bottom of the stairs Eleazer stepped aside with a large stride and a bow, exaggerating the point that they were free to leave. Jeremiah glanced at

Dawson, who nodded, before he turned to the front door and moved on.

Sebastian couldn't let them leave without comment. He moved to block their way, making Florence screech and take a backward step to stand behind Jeremiah, who regained his usual truculence as he glared at Sebastian.

'Move aside,' he muttered.

'So,' Sebastian whispered, 'you signed over your fortune to Dawson in exchange for your family's freedom?'

'Of course. Family is all that matters.' Jeremiah looked him up and down and sneered. 'But a man like you wouldn't understand that. Enjoy your money. We intend to enjoy something that's far more important.'

Jeremiah moved on to consider Temperance, and softened his stern expression.

'Good luck,' Temperance said. 'I hope to see you in Independence soon.'

Jeremiah frowned, his furrowed brow suggesting he was considering and then rejecting several responses.

'So do I,' he said finally. Then he turned to beckon Gabriel to join them.

Sebastian and Temperance said nothing more. Gabriel took his mother's arm and then scurried by without looking at them.

When the family group had merged into the milling customers by the door, Sebastian turned to Dawson, who had now rested a hand on a bulging carpetbag on the counter.

More customers had curtailed their activities to watch the encounter, which was fine with Sebastian as, with Gabriel's unexpected departure leaving their plans in tatters, having witnesses was essential. Walking slowly, Sebastian headed over to the bag and hefted it.

'It's been counted,' Dawson said.

'I trust you,' Sebastian said loudly for the benefit of those near by. 'You have a fine reputation as an honest man.'

Dawson's lips moved with a retort, but when he noted the numerous people who were watching, he bit it back unsaid, perhaps fearing that with nothing to lose, Sebastian would blurt out an accusation. Instead, he gestured to the private gaming room.

'Perhaps before you leave you'd like to enjoy a drink with me.'

'And perhaps another game?'

Dawson smiled widely with a seemingly honest reaction.

'The game started when you rode into Eureka,' he said with a quiet tone for Sebastian's ears only.

Sebastian had no doubt that if they followed Jeremiah and postponed taking on Dawson until another time, Eleazer would follow them and ensure they never got another opportunity to act. So seeing no other option, Sebastian nodded.

He avoided catching Temperance's eye in the hope that she might remain free, but guards moved behind them both and so they headed for the gaming room. Around the entrance hall, the customers returned to their business while the guards ushered them on.

The last time Sebastian had entered

this room, four poker games had been in progress while dozens of customers watched the games. So he headed inside confidently with the bag held over a shoulder, not expecting that Dawson would act when so many people were around, but the moment he looked into the room he came to a sudden halt.

By then it was too late; the guards bundled him forward into the almost deserted room. A swinging door on the other side of the room and the receding sounds of chatter suggested that the area had only just been cleared.

Guards crowded in from behind and he was pushed onwards. So he moved to break into a run, but the two men standing guard on the door opposite closed ranks, ensuring there was nowhere to run to.

Sebastian stopped and, with Temperance at his side, turned to find that eight men had followed them in along with Dawson and Eleazer. To a gesture from Dawson, six of those men spread out around the room, taking positions behind gaming tables and presumably blocking other, unseen exits from the room.

Then the two large guards moved towards them, flexing their fists. Sebastian stood his ground, but before they could tussle, Temperance broke ranks and ran.

Sebastian didn't see how she fared as her movement caused his opponent to turn to watch her and so he used the distraction to hurl the heavy carpetbag at the man's face.

The man thrust up an arm and deflected the bag away. Then, while Sebastian was unbalanced, he swiped the side of his head with a contemptuous blow that sent him to his knees.

The room appeared to sway, although Sebastian's battered senses told him that he was the one swaying. Then he became even more disorientated when his assailant grabbed his collar in one hand, the seat of his pants in the other, and then lifted him bodily off the floor.

He was suspended in the air while still in a kneeling position. Then his assailant raised him to shoulder height and launched him across the room.

Sebastian had a terrifying vision of the ceiling coming closer before the room appeared to tip over. Then he slammed down flat on his back on a table where he lay for a moment before, with a creak and a splintering of wood, the table collapsed and he crashed down onto the floor.

Unable to summon the strength to do anything other than moan he lay within the wreckage and awaited his assailant's next move. That turned out to be the one he feared when the man dragged him to his feet, stood him upright and then rained blows down on his body.

Four quick punches to the chest and face made Sebastian stumble. He started to fall over, but someone had moved behind him and pushed him back upright for the blows to slam into his body again.

Across the room Temperance was being held securely. To his relief she wasn't being beaten and so Sebastian aimed a few punches of his own, but they just sliced through the air. So he was left with trying to roll with the punches and limit the damage.

This worked for a few blows until his assailant caught him with a stinging uppercut to the chin that sent him reeling. This time he wasn't caught and he crashed into another table, tipping it over. He landed on his side and a moment later the table rolled over to slam down on top of him, pinning him to the floor.

'Enough,' Dawson shouted. 'I don't want my precious room destroyed.'

Dawson's men laughed as Sebastian was dragged out from under the table. Then the table was righted and he was placed on a chair. While he gathered his breath and poked at his bruises, Temperance was dragged across the room and deposited on a chair facing him.

As blood streamed from Sebastian's nose and mouth, she shot him a worried glance that acknowledged their hopeless situation. Then Sebastian folded over to rest his head on his arms.

Presently, someone came over and joined them at the table.

Sebastian grumbled at that person to leave, but when a cold towel was pressed down on his cheek he looked up and found that Amelia had joined them. Everyone else had spread out to surround the table while Dawson talked quietly with Eleazer.

The fact that Dawson hadn't had them killed immediately meant he must want something from them and, with Sebastian enjoying a flurry of hope, he sat up and let Amelia dab at the cuts and bruises on his face.

Although she was now dressed as a saloon girl, this job presumably being her reward for double-crossing Jeremiah, he looked into her eyes and tried to force her to look at him. She ignored him and so he whispered to her.

'Help us,' he said.

'I am.' Amelia pressed the towel tightly against his forehead and offered a thin smile.

'You're not. You're doing what Dawson told you to do after you betrayed Jeremiah.'

Amelia sneered, but while she washed the blood off his upper lip, Temperance continued where Sebastian had left off.

'You didn't betray Gabriel, though,' she said.

'He saved my life,' Amelia said with an unconcerned shrug. 'I owed him that.'

'Sebastian saved your life too. What do you owe him?'

Amelia opened her mouth to retort, but their conversation had drawn Dawson's interest and he moved over to the table.

'What were they whispering about?' he asked, dragging Amelia away.

'They wanted to know what you'll do with them,' Amelia said. 'I told them they wouldn't like the answer, but they'd find out soon enough.'

Dawson nodded with approval and then beckoned for one of his men to bring him a six-shooter. Then he sat while all the guards moved in to form a tight circle around the table.

Eleazer drew his gun and sighted Sebastian's head while another man aimed at Temperance's back.

'It's time, Sebastian,' Dawson said around a studied yawn, 'for you to make your offer.'

'What offer?' Sebastian said.

'After running for six months, you returned to the place you were running from. Then you walked in here and did the one thing that was guaranteed to get you killed. You're a gambler. You have a gamble in mind. Tell me what it is.'

'And then?' Sebastian waited, but Dawson's cold gaze gave him no hope of a reprieve and so he tried to think of a ruse that would get them out of their situation. His mind remained blank and so he shrugged. 'I'd hoped we could play poker, as we did six months ago.'

Dawson smiled and then gestured with the six-shooter.

'That's an excellent idea, although I have a more interesting game in mind.'

Dawson flipped open the cylinder and emptied the bullets into his other hand. Then he reloaded one bullet.

With his gaze set on Sebastian, he slipped the gun beneath the table where he thumbed the loaded chamber round, ensuring that Sebastian couldn't see where the bullet ended up.

'What's the gamble?' Sebastian asked when Dawson replaced the gun on the table.

'Whichever one of you takes the gun and shoots the other,' Dawson said, 'gets to live.'

'Never!' Sebastian snapped, while Temperance thumped the table, shaking her head.

'Except you don't know where the bullet is. The next shot might be an empty chamber, in which case you'll both live, or it might be a bullet, in

194

which case one of you will die.' Dawson pushed the gun towards Sebastian. 'Pick up the gun and take the gamble.'

'No.'

Dawson shrugged. 'You could even try to turn the gun on me, although you won't live for long enough to fire . . . or then again you might. That's the gamble.'

Sebastian considered the gunmen surrounding them and then the gun, mentally rehearsing how long it'd take him to turn the weapon on Dawson. He judged that Eleazer would shoot him before he could take aim.

'What do you really want from this?' he asked.

'Six months ago you gambled and beat me at this very table. Now I want to see you sweat it out over the biggest gamble of your life. Pick up the gun.'

Slowly Sebastian did as he'd been ordered. Then he hefted the gun on the palm of his hand. His action made Temperance open her eyes wide, but it didn't concern Dawson and that convinced him that the next chamber was empty.

'Give me your word that you'll allow Jeremiah and his family to leave and I'll take your gamble.'

Sebastian looked at Temperance and received a nod.

'Done,' Dawson said quickly. Then he smiled. 'I already intended to let them go. I need them alive in case of complications later. You sure aren't the formidable gambler I'd thought you were.'

'I'm not, but I still beat you.'

Dawson chuckled. 'You did once, but not this time. Shoot your friend and then walk away. If she lives, she can join you.'

To Dawson's right Eleazer straightened his gun arm, but Sebastian didn't trust Dawson. If he took the gamble, he reckoned Dawson would then pass the gun on to Temperance and the game would start again.

Sebastian slammed the gun down on the table.

'I've beat you again. I refuse to play your game.'

Dawson sighed wearily as if he'd expected this response. Then he pushed the gun across the table to Temperance.

'Your turn,' he said. 'The chamber could be loaded or not. If you shoot, you'll live, but your friend might die.'

Temperance didn't even look at the gun.

'I'm not a gambler,' she said.

'You're not. You look like a woman who likes plain speaking, and I can make you pick up that gun and shoot Sebastian with four words.'

Temperance started to snap back a retort, but Sebastian flinched as he gathered an inkling of Dawson's intent. Temperance considered him and then sat back in her chair.

'Then do it,' she said.

Dawson turned to Sebastian and took his time in replying.

'Sebastian killed your brother.'

'He didn't,' Temperance said, although she narrowed her eyes as she watched

Sebastian's tight-lipped reaction.

'He didn't pull the trigger, but it was his fault. Denver Fetterman hired Sebastian to lead your settlers into a trap.'

'Jeremiah said you weren't to be trusted,' Temperance snapped, glaring at Sebastian. She grabbed the gun and then swung it up to aim at his head.

'Don't listen to him,' Sebastian said, leaning back.

Temperance cocked the gun and straightened her arm.

'Then deny it.'

14

'I can't deny Dawson's claim,' Sebastian said, speaking slowly. 'Denver Fetterman did hire me, but I led you away from danger and not towards it.'

'I'm sure that's a comfort to my brother and the others who got shot up.'

Temperance lowered her head, making Sebastian think she wouldn't fire, but then she snapped her head back up and she drew back the trigger. A hollow click sounded. The noise only appeared to anger Temperance even more and with her eyes blazing, she fired again, and then again.

Click after click sounded and with each failed shot Sebastian's heart thudded, but he couldn't make himself move away as he stared down the barrel of a gun that promised him death within moments.

Dawson chuckled. Only when the sound grew into a hearty laugh did Sebastian's shocked senses tell him that Temperance had already fired six times. She still fired once more before she lowered her gaze, accepting what Dawson had done.

Dawson then opened his hand revealing the bullet he'd palmed.

'You cheated,' Sebastian murmured.

'Of course,' Dawson said. 'Surely you didn't think I'd risk one of you turning the gun on me, did you?'

Sebastian tensed, readying himself to leap at Dawson now that he'd admitted the truth. He didn't expect to get enough time to inflict any damage before Eleazer shot him, but to his surprise it was Temperance who acted first. With a wail of anger she slammed the gun down on the table and then leapt to her feet.

Sebastian scraped back his chair, moving backwards, but he wasn't quick enough to avoid Temperance's wild swipe that clipped the side of his head.

He stumbled to the side and that walked him into a slap to the cheek and then a straight-armed lunge with the palm of her hand that cracked his head back.

Then Temperance was on him. She repaid Sebastian for his supposed crime with fierce blows that drove him on across the room until he tripped over the debris of the broken table and slammed down on his back.

Temperance stood stooped over him, gathering her breath while rolling her shoulders after her exertions. Dawson's men shouted encouragement at her to keep fighting and money even changed hands.

Dawson and Eleazer drew back and eyed the men enjoying the fight as much as they considered Temperance and Sebastian, presumably in case their fight was a ruse. If they'd been able to see Temperance's disappointed expression, they'd have known otherwise.

With a heavy, guilt-ridden heart and with his limbs feeling weary, Sebastian clambered to his feet and then picked his way out of the broken table legs. He raised his arms in defence, but he put up no resistance when Temperance batted them aside and then shoved him on, her flaring eyes defying him to resist.

Sebastian couldn't bring himself to do anything other than back away, but then, behind Temperance, he saw a reason to fight back. Quickly, before anyone else noticed that Amelia was sidling along past the table on an unknown mission, he stopped moving backward and squared up to Temperance.

That was the reaction Temperance had been waiting for and she charged him. Sebastian retaliated with a berserk flailing of his arms that deflected her blows, but in his weakened state they were still powerful enough to unbalance him. He fell on his back where he lay wheezing while the exhausted Temperance knelt and pattered weak punches down on him.

Dawson's men became more strident in their demands for a proper fight. Their derision grew in volume until one man shouted out a warning.

That drew Sebastian's attention and he looked up to see Amelia slipping out through the now-unguarded other door. Clutched under an arm was the carpetbag containing his money.

Sebastian didn't mind seeing his winnings disappear as everyone's attention was then diverted from them.

Dawson shouted for Eleazer to catch Amelia and so Eleazer led a line of men to the door only to find it'd been secured from the other side. Eleazer stood back to let one of Dawson's huge guards put a shoulder to the door, and this activity provided even more of a distraction to those left in the room.

Temperance even stopped slapping Sebastian to watch developments, but Sebastian looked at Dawson. Unfortunately, the moment had already been lost.

Dawson turned to him while backing

away to stand between the two men he'd ordered to stay in the room. Sebastian still stood up and, as the door splintered and the guards spilled out into the corridor, he faced Dawson.

'So that was what you and Amelia were whispering about,' Dawson said.

Sebastian smiled. 'As you said, I wouldn't come here unless I had a plan.'

He said no more as he had nothing left to offer and so, to buy himself a few more moments, he shuffled towards the table where Dawson had played out his gamble.

'Tell me the rest,' Dawson said, 'or I'll make this a long night for you.'

Sebastian offered a thin smile while he thought rapidly. Then his gaze fell on the gun that'd been left on the table. It was lying in front of the chair at which he'd sat, except he was sure that Temperance had put it down before her chair.

The gun could have moved when she'd attacked him, but he'd first noticed Amelia acting suspiciously when she'd been beside the table. Hoping that she had a conscience, after all, he slumped down in the chair from where he considered Dawson.

He opened his mouth, but then winced and felt his jaw as he tried to give the impression that only his discomfort was delaying his reply. With his shoulders hunched, he pushed the gun around in a circle and then, adopting a distracted air, he picked it up.

'Amelia's not the only one here who's working for me,' he said with as much confidence as he could muster.

Then he waved the gun around casually, giving the impression he would point it at whoever was secretly helping him. Dawson's resolute gaze didn't waver.

'You're bluffing,' he said. 'I saw through your bluffs six months ago and I can still read you.'

'Six months ago I won our final game with the better hand.' Sebastian jerked the gun to the side to aim at Dawson's chest. 'And this time I'll win again.'

Dawson considered the gun and then snorted a laugh.

'With an unloaded gun?'

'I'm gambling that it's not.'

Dawson raised an eyebrow. 'You saw me empty the bullets out.'

'And where are those bullets now?'

Doubt flickered in Dawson's eyes and that was enough for Sebastian to risk trusting that Amelia had helped him. He fired.

Despite his resolution, his heart still thudded with delight when gunfire exploded. A moment later, Dawson dropped to his knees with his chest holed and an incredulous expression on his face before toppling over onto his front.

His guards appeared as shocked as Dawson had been that a seemingly unloaded gun was now capable of firing. So, before they got their wits about them, Sebastian fanned wild gunfire to the side.

He fired five more times, each time hearing the welcome blast of gunfire. Thankfully, two of those shots sliced into the guards' chests, making them keel over. One man lay still on his back while the other struggled to raise himself, but he failed when Temperance got over her surprise and hurried across the room.

A swift kick to the jaw poleaxed the injured man. Then she wrested his gun off him and moved on to take the second man's gun.

When she stood up and faced Sebastian, Temperance fingered both guns, her delay in acting showing she was thinking about resolving their confrontation. Then, with a shrug, she underhanded a gun to Sebastian.

'Later,' she said.

Sebastian nodded. 'When we've dealt with Eleazer.'

Temperance frowned, but said no more as she hurried on to the door through which Amelia had run. Sebastian went the other way and tried the door that led back into the entrance room, but it had been locked and so he ran across the gaming room.

At the door he stopped to stretch his battered limbs and consider Dawson's dead body, but the sight didn't lessen his anger at Virgil's brutal death and so he followed Temperance out into the corridor.

Nobody was visible in a long corridor that tracked beside the main entertainment rooms, but along one side numerous doors led into these rooms providing plenty of choices for Amelia's flight.

Temperance looked at Sebastian for a suggestion and so he paused to consider how he reckoned Amelia would act. Then, figuring that she'd find safety in a crowd, he turned towards the saloon, the most occupied part of the building.

Temperance hurried after him and, when he threw open the door, they came out at the back of the bar with the saloon before them. At least a hundred people swarmed around the bar, making it hard to see for more than a few yards and nearly impossible to pick out one woman who would be trying to hide.

'This is hopeless,' Temperance said, speaking loudly enough to be heard over the hubbub.

'Whether she's here or not, we'll never find her.'

Sebastian raised himself to peer over the heads of the customers and then smiled.

'Perhaps it doesn't matter. Eleazer reckons she's in here.'

He pointed and Temperance raised herself onto tiptoes to watch Eleazer lead a group of men around the saloon, questioning the customers. They appeared to get answers as Eleazer moved purposefully to a corner, the crowd thinning out as they passed.

Temperance and Sebastian found an unoccupied section of the bar and clambered over it. Then they tried to barge customers aside. In his weakened state, Sebastian failed to make headway and so instead he wove by people, all the while aiming for a corner he could no longer see.

He became so used to rocking from side to side that when he emerged from the block of men around the bar he stumbled forward; Temperance had the same problem as she missed her footing and walked straight into him. Sebastian righted himself and then, across twenty feet of cleared space to the corner, he saw Amelia along with Eleazer and the rest of the men who had chased after her.

She had yet to notice Eleazer's approach as she was speaking casually with a man, seemingly engaging in routine banter for a customer and a saloon girl to avoid drawing suspicion upon herself. Then they headed towards the door, again acting in a non-suspicious manner, with the man now carrying the bag of money.

Sebastian didn't recognize her aide,

but he presumed that, as when they'd found her, she'd wormed her way into someone's confidence. But it didn't look as if she'd succeed this time as Eleazer directed his men to cut them off. Their movement caught her attention and made her stop.

The few customers around them chose that moment to melt away and, with space opening up rapidly, Amelia looked around for the best direction to flee.

Her accomplice continued to move, seemingly oblivious to the threat, and Eleazer made him pay for his mistake when he drew his gun and blasted lead. His shot thudded into the man's stomach, making him fold over. A second shot to the head downed him.

The man came to rest draped over the bag, while the gunshot spread a wave of silence through the saloon. Eleazer glanced around, providing a calming gesture that said everything was under control.

His steady consideration of the saloon

moved on until it reached Sebastian and Temperance, who he considered with bemusement. His interest caused Amelia to look at them too, and she provided a slight shrug that neither asked for their help nor said that she expected it.

Then, as one, Eleazer's men swung round to face them, their actions making the customers standing behind Sebastian and Temperance scramble away.

'So, has she stopped beating you?' Eleazer asked.

'She has,' Sebastian said, glancing down at the gun he still held aimed downwards, 'to Dawson Breen's regret.'

Sebastian had hoped the hint that his boss had met his end might worry Eleazer, but it made him smirk, perhaps as he weighed up his chances of taking over the empire.

'Boasting about that in a room full of Dawson's friends wasn't a wise move. You'll never leave here alive.'

Whispering sounded around the saloon as the customers picked up on the meaning of their conversation and so Eleazer waved for quiet. Silence descended, but then, from behind the customers, a loud and clear voice yelled out.

'Fire! There's a fire! Everyone, get out!'

15

Despite the desperate, echoing demand that filled the saloon, the customers stood poised, for seemingly an age, although it must have been for only a moment.

Sebastian realized with a start that he recognized the shouter's voice: Jeremiah had returned to help them. Then Gabriel joined in, this time shouting from the other side of the bar.

'The fire's spreading!' he shouted. 'Everyone, run!'

The second demand broke everyone out of their shocked states. Customers surged away from the bar, but the people at the front resisted, not wanting to walk into the middle of a potential gunfight.

Moment by moment they were pushed forward by the frantic people behind them and the space between Sebastian and Eleazer narrowed to create an aisle. Rapidly this took the gunmen on the edges of the line out of Sebastian's view and, with Gabriel and Jeremiah continuing to shout about a fire, Eleazer grunted with anger and raised his gun arm.

With distractions on either side, his gunshot whistled by Sebastian's right ear. Sebastian ignored the chaos and calmly swung up his arm. His single shot thundered into the centre of Eleazer's chest, making him stand up straight with his back arched.

Then Temperance tore a second gunshot into Eleazer's side and he keeled over. The gunfire panicked the customers and they charged for the door, heedless now of the danger.

Before the remaining gunmen were taken from view, Sebastian fired twice. One shot was wild, but the other hit a gunman in the neck while Temperance slammed a deadly shot into another's skull. Then the wave of people swarmed between them and took the rest from his sight.

With people buffeting him from all directions, Sebastian fought to turn and face Temperance.

'Are we bothered about the rest of the gunmen?' he shouted over the rising clamour.

'They probably helped Eleazer attack our people,' Temperance said, 'but the men who gave the orders were Dawson and Eleazer.'

'Agreed.' Sebastian lurched forward as the customers pressed against him. 'Now we just have to get away before the fire spreads.'

Temperance nodded before she too was dragged away. Then they could do nothing other than let the seething crowd draw them along.

Quickly they reached the door without Sebastian seeing Eleazer's body, the remaining gunmen, or Amelia. Neither could he see any sign of the fire Jeremiah and Gabriel had presumably lit.

He surged across the entrance room and spilled out into the harsh light

216

outside where, like the other fleeing customers, he craned his neck while looking back over his shoulder at the building. But he saw no flames or smoke.

A hand clamped down on his shoulder and he spun round to find he was facing Jeremiah.

'Stop looking for the fire,' Jeremiah said with a wink. 'There isn't one.'

'A distraction?'

Jeremiah smiled. 'I figured you stood no chance of getting away without one.'

Jeremiah looked around, presumably for the others, and Sebastian pointed when he saw Temperance emerge from the saloon with Gabriel.

'I'm surprised you came back,' Sebastian said.

Jeremiah shrugged. 'As a father, I have to show my boy the right way to behave.'

★ ★ ★

'Do you expect me to forgive you for what you did?' Temperance asked after

217

she'd explained to the others why she and Sebastian were at loggerheads.

They had drawn up five miles out of town, and Sebastian turned his horse to look back towards Eureka before he replied. So far they hadn't seen anybody pursuing them out of town and, with the confusion they'd left behind outside the saloon, Sebastian was starting to think they might escape, after all.

'I'm not asking you to,' Sebastian said. 'I lied, but even if I'd told the truth, you people would still have gone on to Independence and I'd have still led you along the same route.'

Temperance ground her jaw and then lowered her head, appearing as weary in the moonlight as Sebastian felt. The beating he'd suffered followed by the flight out of town in the cold made him feel every bruise and extinguished his desire to argue. Accordingly, he looked to the others for their reaction.

Florence stayed back and Gabriel wouldn't meet his eye, leaving Jeremiah to move his horse closer. Despite Temperance's revelations about his duplicity, to Sebastian's surprise he considered him with less antipathy than usual.

'I knew something was wrong,' he said, 'from the moment Gabriel caught you sneaking around our wagons.'

Sebastian shrugged. 'That night I was desperate to leave town, but Denver Fetterman didn't give me my ultimatum to betray you until later.'

Temperance muttered something under her breath, but Jeremiah merely frowned.

'Except you didn't betray anyone. You faced a difficult choice in an impossible situation, but the important thing is that in the end, you did the right thing.'

Temperance stared at Jeremiah agog until she nodded slowly, as presumably she understood where his change of heart had come from.

'Just as you did,' she said.

Jeremiah gave a curt nod and then,

with a determined swing of the reins, he moved away. With that most likely being the extent of the agreement they would reach that night, everyone except Sebastian turned their horses to face away from town.

'It's a long journey to Independence,' Jeremiah said after a while.

'That means,' Temperance said, 'we should hole up somewhere for the rest of the night. Then we'll need to travel quickly tomorrow.'

Jeremiah gave an affirmative grunt and then turned to Sebastian, who looked aloft at the stars before he replied.

'I wish you luck with your journey,' he said.

'That mean you're not coming?' Jeremiah asked with a surprising level of concern in his tone.

'After you raised the alarm, we didn't see Amelia again, but I reckon she's the kind of double-crossing snake who'll have escaped with my money.' He smiled. 'She can't have gone far yet.'

Jeremiah shook his head. 'I said before that you faced a difficult situation, but in the end you did the right thing and that's all that matters. It's time to do that again.'

Sebastian blinked hard. 'Are you saying I should let her get away with my money?'

'As I keep telling Gabriel, money can't buy you nothing you need.'

Sebastian couldn't think of an answer to that, but when he noticed how Gabriel was now looking at him, and how Temperance also appeared interested in his response, he gave a slow nod.

'You're right,' he said. He gave Temperance an apologetic look that promised they'd talk later. Then he turned to the long journey to Independence. 'Maybe some dreams don't have to stay lost for ever.'

We do hope that you have enjoyed
reading this large print book.
Did you know that all of our titles
are available for purchase?

We publish a wide range of high
quality large print books including:
Romances, Mysteries, Classics
General Fiction
Non Fiction and Westerns

Special interest titles available in
large print are:
The Little Oxford Dictionary
Music Book, Song Book
Hymn Book, Service Book

Also available from us courtesy of
Oxford University Press:
Young Readers' Dictionary
(large print edition)
Young Readers' Thesaurus
(large print edition)

For further information or a free
brochure, please contact us at:
Ulverscroft Large Print Books Ltd.,
The Green, Bradgate Road, Anstey,
Leicester, LE7 7FU, England.
Tel: (00 44) 0116 236 4325
Fax: (00 44) 0116 234 0205

THE HEAD HUNTERS

Mark Bannerman

Elmer Carrington, former Captain of the Texas Rangers, is the victim of a horrendous crime committed by the Mexican bandit, Mateo. Accompanied by Daniel Ramos, another victim, he sets off in pursuit of the man they hate. Travelling into Mexico, they encounter terrifying hazards, but nothing prepares them for the torture that awaits them when Carrington is given a hideous task. Failure to carry it out could mean death for them both . . .

ROAD TO RIMROCK

Chuck Tyrell

The town of Rimrock lay dying, and its local drunk lay in the gutter, passed out again. As usual, Marshal Matt Stryker puts Stan Ruggart in the hoosegow to sleep off the whiskey like a regular lowlife. But Ruggart has a family, and a fortune. When Ruggart's throat is cut and the will turns up in Stryker's pocket, there are serious problems on the horizon. The marshal needs to keep ahead of three gunmen looking for vengeance, and stay alive long enough to probate the will . . .

THE LONESOME DEATH OF JOE SAVAGE

C. J. Sommers

Family duty leads Tracy Keyes to search for his cousin, the notorious Wyoming bad man Joe Savage. Tracy hasn't seen Savage since they were boys, and isn't sure he'd even recognize his criminal cousin if they met. Being related to the infamous Savage makes things no easier for him, nor do the bounty hunters who dog his trail, believing that Tracy can lead them to the outlaw. By the end of the long journey, Tracy is convinced that he is only following Joe Savage into his own grave . . .

SIX FOR TEXAS

Elliot Long

When Tom Nation is lynched for no good reason, there is only Ed Colerich left alive to take the word back to the T Bar N ranch on the Brightwater. So when six ride back to Texas, they only have two things on their minds: an eye for an eye and a tooth for a tooth. With guns blazing and blood flowing, there isn't one man or woman among them certain to return to the T Bar N alive . . .